"Al Riske's writing is a gift. With uncommon grace and clarity, he arranges the details of our everyday lives into a sort of poetry. In *Sabrina's Window,* seventeen-year-old Joshua and 31-year-old Sabrina are searching for themselves when they find each other, forming a bond that is as unlikely as it is deep and abiding. Reading Riske's novel, I was reminded of how fragile and magnificent we humans are, how silly and petty . . . and absolutely generous we can be."
—*Judy Clement Wall,* Zebra Sounds

"This book invites you in and then shuts the door quietly behind you, allowing you to share moments between characters in a private space with an atmosphere of intimacy that may leave you afraid to breathe for fear of intruding."
—*Douglas Edwards, author of* I'm Feeling Lucky: The Confessions of Google Employee Number 59

"Sabrina's Window is a pure pleasure to read. Al Riske does an excellent job of creating colorful, realistic characters."
—*Paige Lovitt,* Seattle Post-Intelligencer

"Al Riske has packed so much emotional punch in this 217-page slice-of-life novel that I'm still thinking about the people that inhabit the pages . . . Reading it was much like hearing a piece of music. I know I'll read it again, and re-discover the nuances of something beautiful."
—*Katherine Adams,* Goodreads

SABRINA'S WINDOW

AL RISKE

LUMINIS BOOKS

LUMINIS BOOKS
Published by Luminis Books
1950 East Greyhound Pass, #18, PMB 280
Carmel, Indiana, 46033, U.S.A.
Copyright © Al Riske, 2012

Grateful acknowledgment is made to Rosanne Cash for permission to quote from her song
"From the Ashes" © 1990 Chelcait Music (Administered by Measurable Music LLC, a Notable
Music Co.) BMI. All rights reserved. Used by permission.

ISBN-10: 1-935462-53-9
ISBN-13: 978-1-935462-53-8

Printed in the United States of America

10 9 8 7 6 5 4 3 2 1

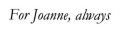

For Joanne, always

Special thanks to:

Gretchen Clark
Dee Elder
Greg Bardsley
Mark Richardson
Rachel Canon
Marian Davis
Karen Croft
Terry McKenzie
Carrie Motamedi
Sue Jenks
Starline Judkins
Greg Moon
Rosanne Cash

My moment of waking, darlin'

Is so close at hand

And I'm gonna rise from the ashes.

—*Rosanne Cash, "From the Ashes"*

1

THE BOY WHO broke Sabrina's window stood on the stoop, shivering. This early in the morning it was still chilly here in the high desert, but he seemed scared, too—like he couldn't imagine anything worse than being right where he was, having done what he did.

Shards of glass bit into the wooden planks beneath his hiking boots.

"I broke your window," he said.

"So I see."

He handed her the *Sunday Journal*.

"I'm really sorry."

"What's this?" Sabrina asked.

He looked up at her then, sleepy-eyed and as confused as she was. The boy had an expressive face. It wasn't hard to tell what he was thinking, and that made her feel sorry for him. More sorry than she already felt.

"Wrong house," he said finally.

She looked up and saw the small pickup idling by the curb, newspapers in the cab, more in the bed. On both sides of the street, practically every house was an adobe with the doors and window frames painted the same blue you see throughout New Mexico. It wasn't too hard to put together, even without that first cup of coffee.

The boy said, "I'm not the regular guy. I'm just . . . I'm filling in, and I got confused. I thought this was a porch-delivery house, and I . . . I threw the paper. I threw it pretty hard, I guess. I should have—"

Sabrina pulled her robe tight around her throat and handed the paper back to the boy. He glanced back at his idling pickup—he hardly seemed old enough to drive—then looked into her eyes.

"I'll pay for the window," he said.

The offer was sincere. She could see it in the boy's face, hear it in his voice. He was ready to take full responsibility but also dreaded the cost, whatever it would be. Sabrina did, too, and yet—

"I'll tell you what," she said. "You can do some things for me *mañana* and we'll call it even."

WHEN JOSHUA MARGOLIS returned to work off his debt, the woman, Sabrina Carlsen, was wearing black jeans and a white tanktop, hoop earrings and a silver bracelet. Her top was untucked and her dark brown hair fell freely around her shoulders. She folded her arms.

"Good, you're here," she said. "We've got a lot to do."

They walked around to the backyard, where she handed him a five-pound sledgehammer.

"I can't stand all this cement," she said. "I want it out of here."

Joshua looked at the gray expanse in front of him.

"Couldn't I just pay for the window?" he asked.

Sabrina laughed and tousled his hair.

"It'll be fun," she said. "I'll be back in an hour or so to help you."

Joshua took a good hard swing with the sledgehammer, then had to look closely for evidence that he had done any damage whatsoever. He tried again. Taking an even bigger swing this time—rocking back and raising up—he brought the hammer head down hard and felt the shock in his hands. Now there were two tiny pock marks in the concrete.

When he looked up, Sabrina was already gone. There was just the hint of her perfume in the air.

ALL WAS QUIET when Sabrina returned. How odd. She squinted at the tiny face of her silver wristwatch. Well, maybe not so odd. It had been three hours since she left Joshua to pound her patio to smithereens.

The patio, she discovered, was still intact, hardly scratched. Under the head of the sledgehammer, there was a note scrawled on the back of a faded and now un-crumpled receipt of some sort, evidently the only scrap of paper available:

"Sorry. Need a bigger sledge. Better yet, a jackhammer."

Sabrina smiled, sighed, folded the note in half, folded it again, kept folding it until she couldn't fold it any more.

"Guess I'll have to call Barry," she said aloud.

BARRY MARTINEZ TENDED bar at Sabrina's favorite watering hole, the Shadow Dance Bar & Grill, and she could tell right away that he was interested. It took her awhile to warm up to him, though. For one thing she was seeing someone else when they met. But Barry began to seem a lot more attractive when she found out he was also an apprentice glassblower. She was a painter herself (and a failed actress, but never mind that). She made her living cutting hair, though, so they were kind of alike. In any case, she had always been drawn to creative people.

Now Barry had his shirt off and his torso was glistening in the slanting sunlight. At his feet, the patio was rubble. Sabrina handed him a cold Pacifico, his favorite.

"I really appreciate this," she said.

He drank half the bottle as Sabrina watched sweat drip from his chin to his chest and run down over his softly rounded belly. In fact there were several small streams cutting through the dust on his body like flash floods after a sudden rainstorm.

"No problem," he said. "You can show me your appreciation in just a minute."

Sabrina just smiled.

Everything she knew about men (well, not everything) she had learned from reading *Esquire* magazine. A longtime subscriber, she understood that men, at their best, had a lot of romanticized notions and wild fantasies about women. The reality was much different, and yet she was not averse to playing into those fantasies from time to time.

She liked thinking of herself as every man's fantasy.

THE BOY HELPED her move the rubble to the side of the house, where each week she would put a few chalky chunks into the garbage (whoever thought to put wheels on garbage cans deserved the kind of thanks Barry got, ten times over, she thought) until it was all gone.

The boy's eyes were dark but bright, and his hair was blond on top but nearly black underneath. She asked him if he had dyed it. He shook his head.

"No, it just does that," he said.

He seemed shy yet open, and her heart went out to him. He was so cute and so sincere—the kind of boy any girl should feel lucky to have, but wouldn't. She got the feeling that he had not yet been hurt. Not deeply. But of course he would be. And the damage . . . she didn't want to think about the damage.

"What are you going to do back here?" he wanted to know.

"Plant grass, a few flowers, maybe have a garden over in that corner."

"Need some help?"

"You've paid your debt," Sabrina said.

She watched Joshua's lip curl and his shoulders bunch together.

"I could help anyway," he said.

Sabrina just looked at him.

"How old are you?" she asked.

"Seventeen. How old are you?"

She mussed his hair, which was becoming a habit.

"Don't get cocky, kid."

"I already have a girlfriend," he said, "if that's what you're worried about."

Sabrina, who was thirty-one, couldn't help but smile.

"Okay, then," she said. "Come back next week and I'll put you to work."

2

SABRINA HAD FALLEN in love with New Mexico instantly and forever. She didn't count the airport or Albuquerque. Albuquerque was just another American city to her. But once she got on to the Turquoise Trail the feeling was much different.

She would always remember driving north in her rented Ford Focus. It was cloudy but warm and the landscape looked a lot like California at first, but as she continued into the hills, everything changed. The ground rose, rocky and dotted with sage brush. Then she rounded a bend and everything was green. A forest of small trees spread out before her. The workplace was all but forgotten.

The land, she noticed, was an odd combination of very flat and very hilly. She stopped along the roadside to retrieve some snacks from the trunk and saw her first arroyo on the other side of a barbed-wire fence where three cows grazed.

She was not in any hurry. She could do whatever she wanted. It was an uncommon feeling, and Sabrina liked it. She decided she would live here as soon as she could.

Sabrina had expected to love Santa Fe, and she did—but not unreservedly. It was the traffic. The traffic reminded her of Los Angeles. And it was hard to find a place to park.

She took the High Road to Taos, the slower, more scenic route, which snakes along a ridge that, much of the time, is higher than anything around it, except the blue mountains on the horizon. There was hardly any traffic that day, and no one seemed to be in a hurry, least of all Sabrina. Even so, she made only one stop—a viewpoint in the Carson National Forest, where the evergreen trees looked roughly as tall as in Washington or Oregon, where she had grown up. Almost everywhere else she had seen here the trees looked notably shorter than what she was used to.

Then, descending into Taos, she knew she had found home. High mountains around a small plain—a nice place to build a town. It was smaller and less sophisticated than Santa Fe but also less pretentious. Perfect.

She had thought she would be inspired living among so many talented people, but mostly she's just been intimidated. Her best painting paled in comparison to the work of New Mexico artists she really admired—Greg Moon, Margaret Nes, Miguel Martinez, R.C. Gorman . . .

SCHOOL WAS OUT, and Joshua could think of no better way to spend the summer than hanging out with Ronni. Her family had this old-style hacienda on the outskirts of Taos, with an aboveground pool in the backyard, and he would drive out there most days. If he wasn't working.

This time, they were sitting at the kitchen table, and she was showing him a new photo album she had convinced her parents to pick up for her on a trip into town. He wasn't expecting any resistance, let alone a fight, when he offered to help her fill it.

"Oh, no, that's okay," Ronni said. "It'd just be boring old family snapshots."

"You didn't think it was so boring going through my family's albums."

"I know. That's what gave me the idea to do this one."

Ronni was the most crazy beautiful girl Joshua had ever dated. The other two couldn't compare. Not with Ronni's long two-tone hair (light and lighter shades of brown, thanks to frequent exposure to the high-desert sun), her bright green eyes, her mischievous grin, her killer body. Even the small gap between her two front teeth added to her charm.

"So what makes you think I wouldn't like to see your pictures?" Joshua asked.

Mrs. Seger, a quiet, efficient woman with the same two-tone hair as Ronni only much shorter, opened a cupboard and pulled out an old shoe box.

"Now's the perfect time to get started," she said, sliding the box onto the scarred wooden table between them.

Ronni reached for it, but Joshua was quicker.

"What's the matter?" he said. "Got a little bare-bottom shot in here you don't want me to see?"

"Come on, Joshua, this is embarrassing."

"Like my face wasn't red when you were giggling over that one of me—"

Ronni scooted to the edge of her seat, leaned forward.

"That was different," she said

"Yeah, it was me then. Now it's your turn," he said, lifting the lid off the tattered box—one corner held together by brown packing tape.

"Joshua, if you do . . . "

"What?"

"I'll never speak to you again," Ronni said.

Her father, a stern-faced sheriff's deputy, came into the kitchen and snagged a Dos Equis from the fridge.

"Go ahead," he said. "She's bluffing."

"He won't because he knows I mean business," Ronni said, without taking her eyes off Joshua.

Mr. Seger twisted the cap off his cerveza and stared briefly into Joshua's eyes, then went back to the baseball game playing on the big black Trinitron in the corner of the family room. Mrs. Seger followed with a bowl of corn chips and, in passing, patted Joshua's shoulder and smiled.

"I'm warning you," Ronni said.

Joshua peered into the box.

"I'm not talking to you if you do," she said.

He looked up.

She pursed her lips and came out of her seat slightly; Joshua twisted sideways and held the box just out of reach. She sat back down.

Random incidents flashed through his mind: Being in her room and having her say, "You don't have to leave, just turn around," as she changed her clothes. Her saying, "That's what you think, Homie," when he claimed he would never change a dirty diaper. But now, watching him across the kitchen table, she wasn't saying anything.

Joshua stood, toppling his chair behind him, and dropped the box on the table. The contents bounced and mostly landed back in the box, but a few stray snapshots landed on the table. He turned then and stumbled on the overturned chair. He tried to pick it up, set it right, but it moved away from him somehow, his foot and his hand working at cross purposes.

Embarrassed, he gave up and walked out. Ronni followed, stifling a laugh.

"Oh, don't leave mad," she said. "If it means that much to you . . ."

The glare outside made his eyes water, but he kept going.

"Come back inside," she said.

He couldn't even look at her now, just jumped in his pickup, slammed the door with a tinny bang, and fired up the engine, giving it more gas than he meant to. As he drove away, he looked in the rearview mirror and saw Ronni standing in the driveway, hands on her hips.

WHEN HE GOT back to his house, he kept going and ended up at Sabrina's place—a location he would find his way to more and more. Though he hadn't given it much thought, he was vaguely aware of a strong, instant, inexplicable bond between them. It was as if he had already known her a long time, though

11

of course he hadn't—unless it was in some other lifetime and he didn't really believe in that.

"Hey you," she said. "You want to come in? We're just watching the game."

He could hear someone in the living room yelling, "Going, going . . . damn!"

"No, I . . . "

"What?"

"Want me to weed the flowerbed?"

He looked at her and saw that she was looking back at him as if he were a puzzle she couldn't figure out.

"If that's what you're dying to do," she said.

Joshua felt his lips turn up at the corners then and was surprised to find he was almost sort of smiling.

"Well, you've got a lot of weeds here," he said.

Sabrina smiled, too. Just a little.

"I see what you mean," she said. "I'll come out and help you in a minute."

When she knelt down beside him, she said, "So, what's really going on?"

"I just had a fight with my girlfriend."

She nodded to herself and dug up a weed.

"A bad one?"

He nodded to himself, too.

"What about?"

Joshua stared at the ground and shook his head.

"This is going to sound stupid . . . "

"Why should you be any different?" Sabrina said.

Joshua looked up.

"I just mean it's always something stupid," she said. "Every fight I've ever had anyway."

As he told the story, all of it came flooding back to him: Ronni's smug certainty, her father's evident disappointment, her mother's pity, his own wavering weakness, his barely averted impulse to give in to her the way he always did—all that and a bunch of other crazy, blissful, and frustrating crap from the past few months. Now he was left with just that final image of Ronni in his rearview mirror, hands on hips, so crazy killer beautiful and yet . . .

He was grateful for Sabrina's silent interest.

"Good for you," she said at last.

"Good? How is this good?"

"You stood up for yourself, showed some cojones," she said.

Joshua shrugged, uncertain, and Sabrina mussed his hair.

"You have to make a stand sometime," she said. "Even if it seems like a half-assed time for it."

JOSHUA WAS IN his room, a blue bedroom at the front of the house, with two windows that came together in the far corner. The smaller one faced the driveway; the bigger one, the street. Just now the streetlight on the other side flickered to life and cast a yellow glow through his blinds.

He was doing sit-ups. Fifty. A hundred. He kept going, tried not to think. His stomach hurt. He kept going. One hundred and fifty.

"You don't have to leave, just turn around."

He had never done so many sit-ups, never imagined he could. On his back, he stopped, tried not to think. One more. One more and he was sure he'd collapse into unconsciousness.

"That's what you think, Homie."

Though he was winded now and breathing through his mouth, the musty odor of his own tennis shoes, lying on the floor next to him, still seeped into his nostrils. He picked them up and threw them across the room.

"I stink," he said.

Joshua fell back on the floor and remembered his jacket, the faded denim thing Ronni had borrowed and still had. She loved that jacket and he loved seeing her in it, but he didn't want to give it up, either. Would he have to ask her for it? No, she would return it. She wouldn't want to wear it anymore, would she? Would he?

Then he heard the sudden, too-loud ring of the phone—just once—followed by the gentle rumble of his father's voice:

"Joshua! For you!"

In the kitchen, he picked up the phone, a bulky black wall unit with push buttons arranged in a circle to resemble an old-time dial. Joshua lifted the heavy handset off the counter where his father had left it.

"Hello?"

"Are you still mad?"

It was Ronni.

His father opened the oven and suddenly the kitchen was filled with the aroma of a once-frozen lasagna that was now ready to eat. Joshua held up one finger and stepped out into the garage, the door closing behind him until it pinched the hand-set's extra-long cord. All of which would have been unnecessary if his father didn't go in for old-style telephones, radios, flash-lights, and all that other stuff he ordered from Restoration Hardware. Forget about cell phones. They made you too con-nected, he said, and too dependent on others to get you out of trouble you shouldn't get yourself into in the first place.

"No," Joshua said, "but I'm glad you called."

"Because you wouldn't have, right?"

He sat down on the cold concrete step.

"Right."

3

SABRINA WANDERED OVER to her favorite café, a small place on a side street, where she ordered a cold drink—half tea, half lemonade—and took it out on the back patio, which you would never imagine even existed unless you came inside. Even then you might not notice. You might need the girl behind the counter to point it out to you, as had been the case with Sabrina.

It was cool back there under the shade of a mature aspen. A bunch of long-haired guys were reading books, smoking cigarettes, talking, watching over a small child. One played an old Guns 'N' Roses tune on his guitar.

Too late, she noticed Wheeler was among them.

Wheeler Simmons was one of the nicest guys she had ever dated. Also one of the biggest jerks.

He caught her eye, nodded. She smiled, a little, and sat down at one of the weathered wooden tables facing off at an angle.

Smoke from the cigarettes drifted into her eyes and she waved it away, though it smelled good as it sometimes did, depending on the brand. She didn't know which brand smelled good to her and didn't want to know. She opened her book and started reading or at least pretended to be reading.

The screen door separating the café from the courtyard creaked open and banged shut. Sabrina raised her eyes. Her friend Tara was supposed to meet her here twenty minutes ago, but there was still no sign of her.

"All alone today?"

She felt a warm hand on her shoulder, bare except for the narrow strap of her favorite summer dress—bright red cherries on a white background—and she looked up at Wheeler.

Damn those blue eyes.

Sabrina tried to speak, had to clear her throat.

"Looks that way," she said.

His expression. Was that pity? Sadness? Regret? All of the above?

"What are you reading?"

She showed Wheeler the cover of the novel.

"*Rapture.* Any good?"

"Yeah, I'm enjoying it."

"What's it about?"

She felt her face go red and she laughed.

"It's about a blow job."

He smiled.

Damn that smile.

"The whole book?"

She glanced down at the slender paperback, saw she was nearly done.

"Looks that way."

JOSHUA WALKED RONNI home after the evening service at his church. Well, it was her church, too, now. Her family wasn't religious, but she joined him every Sunday. It wasn't far.

"Why is it," she asked, "that I never understand half of what Pastor Daniels says?"

"What didn't you understand?"

"The sermon."

"Oh, is that all?"

"I thought last week was bad, but this week—this week the only thing I understood was what he said about not casting pearls before swine. And that made me feel like . . . oink, oink."

Joshua laughed and shook his head. There was plenty he didn't understand, either—more than he cared to admit, even to himself—but just now they were back at Ronni's place. His trusty ten-year-old Chevy S-10 was out front on the street where he'd parked it when he came to get her.

"Let's go get a pizza," he said.

The best part about church was that he got to see Ronni in a skirt, and he wanted to prolong the experience.

"I haven't got any money," she said.

"No problem. I'm loaded."

"No, you should save your money."

"Save it for what?"

Ronni shrugged.

"Whatever you want," she said.

What Joshua wanted was a pepperoni pizza with onions and olives, but he didn't press it.

"Are you okay?" he asked.

Ronni hopped up on the hood of the freshly washed and waxed pickup, her three-tiered skirt riding high on her thighs. Joshua joined her, though the maneuver made him wince, his stomach muscles still complaining from all the sit-ups he had done.

"I need to find a job," she said.

"School just let out last week. You'll find one soon enough."

"Not if my dad doesn't teach me to drive. He keeps saying I'll wreck the car. It's a big joke to him."

"They all say that. My dad used the same line on me."

"Yeah, when? When you were fifteen and got your learner's permit? Get real, Joshua, I'm seventeen and I'm still getting around on a bicycle."

"Hey, I still put a lot of miles on my bike."

"Yeah, but you have a choice."

He couldn't argue with that.

They looked out across an open field to the Sangre de Cristo range along the horizon. A breeze started to blow and he put his arm around her for warmth. His and hers.

Then, out of nowhere, she said, "You know, Joshua, that's one thing I really like about you. I can say anything to you and I know you won't laugh at me."

As it got colder and the sky darkened, she jumped down and said, "I'd better go in."

Joshua kissed her good night and opened the driver's door.

Before he could get inside, though, Ronni pushed him against the rear side panel and held him there, kissing him again with parted lips. When he pulled back, she stood on her toes and stretched her neck until their lips met again.

THE NEXT DAY, Sabrina ran into her so-called friend, Tara Baker, a busty redhead whose tresses were as curly as ramen noodles. The deep red shade had been Sabrina's suggestion the very first time Tara had come into the salon, and she was right: The color suited her.

"What happened to you yesterday?" Sabrina wanted to know.

"What do you mean?"

"You were supposed to meet me at the café."

"Oh, right. I saw you with Wheeler, so . . . "

"So, what? You just left me there?"

They were in Taos Plaza, the town square, which was basically a small plot of land—a little grass, a few trees, some benches, a statue—surrounded by old adobe shops and galleries. Tara opened the back of her car, one of those boxy Scions, all in white, and put her shopping bags inside before answering.

"Well, yeah, I figured you wouldn't want me getting in the way."

"In the way of what? Me embarrassing the hell out of myself?"

"Why would you be embarrassed? You knew each other pretty well as I recall."

"I didn't know him as well as I thought I did," Sabrina said.

"But you still have feelings for him."

"I don't."

"Oh, come on, Sabrina. I know you do."

Tara got in her car. Sabrina gave up.

"All the more reason not to leave me there by myself," she said, "like I have no friends and nothing to do with myself."

JOSHUA DROVE RONNI out on a quiet country road, past the farms and ranches, past one last broken-down corral, to where the land was barren but for patches of sage brush. He pulled off to the side and got out of the pickup. This would be their last day together for a couple of weeks, as Ronni and her family were leaving on vacation.

"You drive," he said.

"What?"

"You heard me."

She scooted behind the wheel; he walked around and got in through the passenger door.

"Not afraid I'll wreck it?"

He was, actually, but he wasn't about to tell her that. He wasn't stupid.

"Foot on the brake," he said, "and put it in drive."

"It's not like I haven't seen this done a million times, you know."

"Right, well, seeing and doing are two different things."

Ronni smiled indulgently, shook her head, and swept her long hair behind her shoulders. She was wearing a pale blue V-necked T-shirt that he really liked on her.

"Typical male," she said.

Joshua had often been teased for being quick to cry as a boy, so he realized he should probably take "typical male"—a phrase Ronni had been using more and more—as a compliment. Instead, it made him feel stupid, predictable, and small. He stopped telling her what to do and just let her drive. She didn't need his help.

"What's wrong?" she asked.

"Nothing. You're doing fine."

"Come on, something's bothering you."

He was silent.

"You want to tell me about it?"

"It's just . . ."

She took her foot off the gas, coasted to a stop on the shoulder, and waited.

"Enough with the 'typical male' comments already," he said.

"That's what's bugging you? Joshua, I've been saying that for weeks."

"I know."

She shifted into Park.

"So why didn't you say something?"

"I didn't want to make a big deal out of it," Joshua said.

"But it bugged you?"

"Well, yeah."

"I wish you would have told me. It's just something my mom says to my dad sometimes, to tease him."

"Like I said, not a big deal."

"Well, I feel bad."

"It's okay. Don't worry about it."

"Tell me sooner next time, okay?"

"Sure."

She touched his shoulder and looked in his eyes.

"Will you?"

"I will," he said, but he wasn't at all sure that he would.

HERE WAS THE thing: Ronni always had an opinion. Always spoke her mind. He liked that, and then again he didn't.

She said things that threw him off balance.

She said, "I always wished I were a boy."

He knew that she had been somewhat of a tomboy when they were growing up, though no one would guess from the way she looked now. She had grown into a well-endowed young woman. A well-endowed young woman with a mischievous grin and an unusually deep voice. A very sexy voice, Joshua thought. At least he did at first. Now he had mixed feelings. The grin could throw him, too. Like when she said, "You have nice legs—better looking than mine."

First of all, not true.

Second, how was that supposed to make him feel?

Then, when she said things like that, he would remember the thing he wanted to forget: He is six years old, visiting Mexico with his mother. They are staying with his Aunt Selma, who has a daughter his age, Christina. It's a hot day and Christina says he would be cooler in a dress. Would he like to try one of hers? His mother and aunt smile at him, waiting to see what he will say. They are all wearing brightly colored dresses. A soft breeze ruffles through their red, yellow, and blue hems in turn, and he wonders what that would feel like.

4

JOSHUA DIDN'T REALLY like beer, unless of course it was a dry, dusty, high-desert day and the beer was really cold. Then okay, yes, a beer would be good. Two would be better. Three would be great.

Besides, he understood that it was an acquired taste, and the sooner he acquired it, the better he would fit in with the crowd he was now hanging with. Student journalists. Reporters like him, editors, columnists, sportswriters—even an ad rep or two. They were his occasional compadres, a little wilder than his regular friends, but he liked them and they were nice enough to invite him on this little camping expedition, so, great, he had nothing better to do with Ronni out of town.

They had pitched one huge tent and a couple of smaller ones, and now they were all sitting around on rocks, stumps, and fallen logs near a small creek.

"*Otro cerveza?*"

"*Sí.*"

Bradford Grossman, who would be the new editor-in-chief when school resumed in the fall, was one of those guys who had to shave every day. Twice, he said, if he had a date that night. In any case, he looked years older than Joshua and all the other students for that matter—old enough to buy beer without being carded, in fact. He was also the only one who had thought to bring a folding chair, so he looked supremely comfortable next to a massive red-and-white ice chest. He handed Joshua a long-necked bottle.

"What's that you're reading?" Joshua asked.

"Hemingway."

Bradford showed him the cover of *For Whom the Bell Tolls*.

"Ever read it?"

"Can't say that I have."

"You should," Bradford told him. "Check it out."

Joshua took the proffered paperback and read the opening lines about the pine-needled floor of the forest, the wind in the tops of the trees.

"Good choice," he said.

"The man was amazing."

Joshua nodded. He had a healthy respect for Hemingway, but liked other writers better. Not that he would ever say so in front of Bradford.

"He started out as a newspaper reporter, you know."

Joshua said, "*Toronto Star*, right?"

Bradford nodded as he lit up a fat cigar.

That might have been the end of it if not for Dana Tierney. A skinny blonde with a sunburned face, Dana wrote a scathing political column for the school paper, and she happened to be helping herself to an ice-cold Tecate just then.

"Hemingway was full of shit," she said.

Classic Tierney, he thought. Always ready to mix it up, take a contrarian stance. In this case, he wasn't even sure she meant what she said as he thought he saw the hint of a smile cross her lips, just for a moment.

She was mischievous—he liked that—but also a bit intimidating.

Others soon joined the debate, which allowed Joshua to simply kick back and enjoy the show. He liked their passion but didn't really share it. He liked to write and had a talent for telling people's stories, but he wasn't political like the other reporters and he wasn't particularly opinionated—not like Bradford and Dana and the more gonzo types. On the other hand, he liked to think that gave him an advantage. Journalists were supposed to be objective, after all, even if no one really believed they could be.

Before long, people were making the same points over and over again without even realizing it, and Joshua was able to slip away and find a comfortable spot by a fallen tree, where he could watch the sun go down behind the creek, the babble of voices mixing with the babble of water running over rocks.

It was dark when Dana sat down hard beside him, bumping her shoulder into his and leaving it there.

"Hey, there," she said.

"Hey," he said.

She handed him a fresh cerveza. He took a long drink.

"What's with the lone wolf act, Margolis?" she said.

"Lone wolf? Me?"

"Yeah, you," she said. "Does that really work on other girls?"

THEY TURNED THE ground with a rented Rototiller and stood back to admire their handiwork. Actually, Sabrina had done most of it. Joshua's head hurt and he moved unsteadily.

"If I didn't know better, I'd think you were hung over," Sabrina said.

"I may have had a Tecate or two while camping last night."

"Joshua!" She punched him on the shoulder. "I thought you were a nice boy."

"What? I bet you drank when you were in high school."

Sabrina scratched her head vigorously with all ten fingers and shook out her shaggy mane.

"Everyone who drank just got themselves into trouble," she said.

"Tell me about it."

"What did you do?"

"One of the girls there took a liking to me, I guess, and we made out for a while," he said. "Until I had to throw up."

"That does tend to spoil the mood."

In the next yard, a short black-haired woman shook out a wet white shirt and stretched to clip it next to a pair of faded blue jeans on her clothesline.

"I don't know how I'm going to tell Ronni," Joshua said.

"Ronni's your girlfriend?"

Joshua nodded. He was still watching the woman hang her laundry out to dry, idly wondering whether she was worried about the environment or just the size of her electric bill.

"Don't tell her," Sabrina said.

A bead of sweat ran down Joshua's forehead, along one eyebrow, and down the side of his face.

"Don't?"

"Don't."

5

Wheeler Simmons was the first person Sabrina met when she moved to Taos. She didn't know about his reputation. She only knew that he was looking at her—his eyes followed her everywhere—and if she looked at him he would smile. She would smile, too, but look away quickly and continue to wander through the gallery, which had once been someone's house.

He had jet black hair down to his shoulders, a neatly trimmed beard, and startling blue eyes. He was almost too good-looking, she thought. Almost.

She could tell from the fit and fabric of his clothes that he had money, so she figured he was a tourist looking to take home some art. Home would be southern California, she figured.

"See anything you like?" he asked.

"Lots," she said. "How about you?"

"Everything in here is to my liking."

Sabrina smiled.

"Ah, but what will you take home?" she said.

He thought about that for a second, started to say something, but stopped and started again.

"There's no more room at home," he said. "That's why I bought this place."

Sabrina hid her surprise—or tried to—and turned her attention back to the painting on the wall in front of them.

"You have good taste," she said.

"Perhaps there's something you'd like to take home?"

There was, yes, but had she known that Wheeler had already bedded nearly every eligible woman in town, maybe she would have thought twice about doing it.

Maybe.

WHEN RONNI RETURNED, Joshua took her out for pizza at a little place where the walls were painted tomato-sauce red and they served fantastic pies from a wood-fired oven—like nothing he'd ever tasted.

She slipped off her sandals and rested her feet in his lap so he could hold them, as he always did, to keep them warm.

For some reason his mind drifted back to gym class. Being picked at random to lead calisthenics before the coed volleyball games got underway. Girls in loose-fitting tops bending over to touch right hand to left foot, left hand to right foot, while he kept his head up just enough. Ronni catching his eye and chuckling. She knew what he was up to. She started wearing tighter tops after that, but she never said anything, and the other girls never caught on.

"When did you first start liking me?" she asked.

"About seventh grade."

"I mean when did you *really* start liking me?"

"Seventh grade."

He scooted closer, lifted his shirt, and placed her chilly feet against his warm belly. She smiled, closed her eyes.

"Well, when did you finally decide you were going to ask me out?"

"Honestly?"

"I know. I'm being nosy. You should be used to it by now."

"I wanted to for a long time, but I didn't decide to do it until I did it."

"You know, it's really very funny when you find out what people are really thinking about you but they're not telling you. I never would have guessed. I thought you and Tia were together then."

"We were just friends."

"It kind of makes you wonder, doesn't it, who might be thinking those things about you right now but you don't know it."

He wasn't going to tell her, but at the end of the evening, parked in the driveway to her house, he went against Sabrina's advice.

"While you were away, I went camping with some friends. There were a bunch of girls there," he said, "and . . . "

"It's okay, Joshua. I understand."

"Nothing happened really, but Dana Tierney and I sort of…"

"I like Dana. She's cool."

Joshua wasn't expecting that. No way. I like Dana? She's cool? He struggled to continue his half-constructed confession.

"We just, um . . . "

Ronni stopped him.

"It's okay. I'm not mad," she said.

"Really?"

"Really."

She slid across the seat and got out of the car. Joshua got out, too, and walked her to the door.

"Actually," she said, "it makes me feel better about some of the thoughts I've been having lately."

She kissed him and went inside.

JOSHUA AND SABRINA were in the backyard of her two-bedroom adobe, planting seedlings in her garden.

Joshua said, "I'm an idiot."

Sabrina said, "Am I supposed to disagree?"

"Ha! I don't think so. Not this time."

"Why? What'd you do?"

"I told her."

"Told her?"

"You know, about the camping trip."

Sabrina packed the ground around a new strawberry plant.

"The camping trip, right. The one where you were locking lips with what's her name?"

The boy nodded.

"You are an idiot."

"My point exactly," he said.

"After I told you —"

"Yup."

Sabrina sat back on her heels, took off her gloves.

"Why?" she said.

Joshua shrugged. Sabrina felt herself getting angry.

"Conscience get the best of you?" she said. "Couldn't stand lying to her?"

She stopped and stared into Joshua's eyes. He looked away, looked at the dirt.

"Sorry," she said. "I'm not angry with you. I'm mad at an old boyfriend who told me he was with another woman."

"You wish he hadn't?"

"Yes."

She felt a breeze blow along her sweat-damped arms and looked up to see a cloud block the sun. The weather changed so fast here it could be raining in another minute.

"But isn't it important to be honest?"

"Guys always think that. After they've been dishonest."

"Good point."

Sabrina wiped her brow, put her gloves back on.

"So, what happened? Did she break it off?"

"Did you?" Joshua asked.

"Yes."

The boy dug another hole with his spade.

"Ronni was more understanding," he said. "Too understanding."

THEY RAN INSIDE to get out of the rain, but it had already stopped by the time they made it through the back door.

They looked at each other and shrugged.

"Let's just take a break," Sabrina said.

She pointed Joshua into the living room, and he could now hear her cracking ice and pouring drinks in the kitchen.

He had never spent any time in her living room before. He liked it. Tile floor, hand-woven rug, worn leather sofa, the same sort of viga-and-latilla ceiling that his father loved so much, kiva-style fireplace in the corner . . .

From the CDs stacked beside her stereo he could see that she liked Shakira, Jack Johnson, Beck, David Grey, The Wallflowers, Feist, Death Cab for Cutie, Keith Urban, and Rosanne Cash. Except for the country stuff, she had pretty good taste.

What really caught his eye, though, was a massive painting, a colorful abstract dreamscape that reminded him of a hot-air balloon ride he had taken as a little boy. Which was odd because he was pretty sure he had never set foot in a hot-air balloon.

Sabrina handed him a glass; he kept looking at the painting.

"Where'd you get this?" he asked.

"That? It's one of mine."

"One of yours? You mean you painted this?"

"I did. Yes."

"Wow," he said. "You're really good."

"Well, I wouldn't say that, but that one did turn out halfway decent."

Joshua turned to look at Sabrina. She was wearing black jeans and a white tanktop again—her signature look, he was beginning to realize.

"Halfway?" he said. "Are you kidding? It's awesome."

"Thanks."

"I didn't know you were an artist."

"Isn't everyone in Taos?"

"Practically. Yeah. But you're totally talented."

"You're sweet," she said, "but I'm afraid my stuff doesn't really compare to what I've seen in galleries around town."

"You're just being modest."

6

IN A NEW bra top and cropped leggings, Sabrina sat cross-legged on the grass in her backyard, doing her best approximation of the lotus position. Back straight, chin down, palms resting face up on her knees.

Breathe in, breathe out.

It was a lush and somehow fragile evening, everything tinged in twilight blue, pinion incense in the air. She should savor this, she thought, before it all changes.

Breathe in, breathe out.

It was dark. More thoughts sprang up in her mind. She watched them come as she inhaled, go as she exhaled.

There were images of Joshua, Wheeler, Barry, her father . . .

Breathe in, breathe out.

Her father was critical of her work. Always. No flaw overlooked. Ever. Good for the work? Perhaps. Good for the confidence? Hardly.

Breathe in, breathe out.

There was Barry, polite and reserved. She could tell he was just waiting for the chance to do her a favor, show her his superior strength, knowledge, skill. Fuck his superiority, she thought. I hate that shit.

Breathe in, breathe out.

Again.

Again.

Again.

She let her lungs empty slowly, rested easy, and let them fill back up on their own.

JOSHUA DIDN'T SAY anything but he felt a pain down low in his abdomen while working in Sabrina's backyard. He thought it might be a hernia or something. It turned out to be his appendix.

The doctor said if he had waited much longer it would have burst, but as it was he was going to be just fine.

His father was there, too, when he woke up in his hospital bed.

"Ronni looked especially nice today, don't you think?"

Joshua was confused.

"Ronni?"

"She was just here," his father said. "You spoke to her. You don't remember?"

Joshua shook his head.

"What did I say?"

"That's what she asked me."

"Huh?"

"I'm afraid neither one of us could understand you, son."

"Did she say anything?"

His father reached out and brushed Joshua's hair off his forehead. There was a tenderness in his touch and in his eyes—a sort of sadness that was always there, even when he smiled as he now did.

"Get well," he said. "She said she wants you to get well."

Joshua smiled and drifted backward, falling by imperceptible degrees into a deep sleep.

When at last he woke up again, no one was there except an old man asleep in the next bed. Then a nurse appeared. Bright-eyed and beautiful, she pulled the white curtain around Joshua's bed as she strode into the room.

"Buenos dias," she said. "It is time for your bath."

Joshua didn't understand.

"Bath?"

"Sí," she said. "I will wash you."

"Oh."

The nurse smiled and winked. Maybe. Possibly. Or not. He wasn't sure.

"Is that okay?"

"Uh, sure."

He sat up and she removed his hospital gown but left the bedding around his waist. He had been shaved for the operation and was practically hairless down there, which made him feel even younger than he really was. Like a little boy, actually. He tried not to think about that or about how pretty the nurse was.

He could not think about that. No way. Not for a minute. Not one second.

The wet cloth she used was warm on his arms, shoulders, neck, and chest. When she got down to his belly—think history, geography, baseball, anything but—she rinsed the cloth in a basin of warm water she'd brought with her.

"Here," she said, "you do the rest."

"Oh," he said again.

The nurse smiled as she handed him the cloth.

"That was not so bad, eh?" she said.

SABRINA WAS GLAD to see the boy again. She had missed him without realizing it. Now he was back, without his appendix. She said she was sorry, she hadn't known. He waved her off and started telling her about his hospital stay.

She got a kick out of hearing him talk about the nurse. It was something she could easily imagine doing herself. Poor Joshua.

"Why would she do that?" he asked

"She was just having a little fun with you," Sabrina said.

"Right. A little fun at my expense."

She watched the boy's face and knew that the nurse must have been watching it, too, noting the changing shades of confusion, hope, and desire.

"Oh, come on, you should be flattered."

"You think?"

Sabrina mussed his hair.

"She thought you were cute."

WHEN THEY WERE together, Wheeler had brought her flowers, had taken her to the best restaurants in town, then the best restaurants in Santa Fe. He flew her to San Francisco to hear a singer he knew she liked and they spent the weekend at the Mark Hopkins, ordering room service and enjoying the view from the top of Nob Hill. The fog the city is so famous for never showed up when they were there.

He said he liked her paintings and she gave him one, which he hung in his bedroom in place of a much better one, worth two or three thousand dollars, which he very casually gave to her. He encouraged her to paint more and talked of staging an exhibition of her work.

He was exceedingly friendly and everyone loved him, especially women. They all smiled at Sabrina knowingly.

She liked riding around in his car, a classic '57 Thunderbird convertible, turquoise with a black interior. Not that he drove it often. It was fifty years old, after all. But he liked to take it out on special occasions, like the first day of summer, a full moon, or whenever Sabrina finished a painting. Didn't matter that she often finished a single painting several times, going back to it again and again to add new touches (though she had to be careful because one flourish too many could ruin it). He told her the car was named for a Southwestern Indian god of rain and prosperity. Of course.

It was like they were famous. In a way they were. Well, he was.

Then he made a mistake. It was, no doubt, the same mistake he had been making all his life. A very common mistake, actually. He didn't realize what he had, and he ruined it.

40

He disappeared for two days and she knew what was happening, but told herself it didn't matter. Boys will be boys. She would let it slide. She really thought she could. Then he told her—he just had to tell her—and that was the beginning of the end. She wanted to let it slide but she knew deep down that she wouldn't be able to.

She thought it was selfish of him to tell her.

7

LEO DOMINGO, ONE of Joshua's oldest friends, ventured out on the longest limb of the cottonwood tree and jumped. Holding his knees to his chest, he dropped ten feet and smacked into a deep spot in the creek that ran through his family's farm (their own secret swimming hole), sending up a huge splash. When he popped back up, he swam straight for shore. This was the hottest day of the summer so far, but the water was cold.

"You guys need to get more sun," he said. "I think I'm darker than either of you this year."

For comparison, he held his arm up next to Joshua's, then Ronni's. He was indeed darker than either of them.

"Sure, but you're naturally dark," Ronni said.

"No, I'm not. Look—"

Leo turned and pulled his baggy blue trunks down in back to show his tan line, only he pulled them down so far that, without realizing it, he was showing the start of his hairy crack.

Joshua said nothing, but Ronni evidently caught the look on his face. He hadn't even realized he was making a face until she caught his eye. She didn't say anything about it, though.

Joshua didn't see much of Leo during the summer because he was always working on the farm, and it felt a little strange to be seeing him now with Ronni. It used to be Leo and Ronni, with Joshua tagging along every once in a while. Did she still have feelings for Leo? After all, Leo was the one who had broken it off. Or was it possible that someone would actually choose Joshua over his better looking, more athletic, super charming, outgoing friend?

There's a first time for everything, he thought.

He hoped.

Later, when he and Ronni were alone, she told him to lighten up.

"I've seen boys' butts plenty of times. I've got two brothers, remember?"

"How could I forget?"

"Leo has a smokin' bod and he should show it off," she said. "But of course so do you and the same advice applies."

She smiled and so did Joshua. He struck a bodybuilder pose and she swooned.

Over his boney bod.

Very funny.

SABRINA WAS HAVING one of those days when every little thing seemed to go wrong, and then Joshua knocked on her door—it had surprised her at first how often he showed up, silently on his bike (the distance between their homes too long to walk, too short to drive, he said), but now she was used to it.

"You know anything about computers?" she asked.

"A little. Why?"

"For some reason I can no longer print from mine."

"Let me have a look."

He sat down at her kitchen table/desk and started poking around on her sleek silver laptop. She started to relax. It was cute how intensely focused he was. He looked younger than seventeen but acted older, sounded older, seemed older. Perhaps he was an old soul. Without thinking Sabrina reached out and massaged the boy's scalp.

He sat perfectly still.

After a minute, she stopped and said, "Any ideas?"

"Oh, I fixed it," he said. "Your print queue was stopped for some reason."

"Were you ever going to tell me?"

"I didn't want you to stop," he said. "My mom used to do that."

"She doesn't anymore?"

"Well, no, she's, um . . . dead."

"Oh, God, I'm sorry. I had no idea."

"It's okay," he said. "It was like two years ago. I'm, you know, mostly over it."

SABRINA KNEW WHAT it was like to lose your mother far too soon. Hers had been hiking, alone, in Zion National Park, two days after a rain storm. The trails were still slick and she had fallen off a sheer cliff. Hikers on a lower trail found the body a week later. Sabrina was a freshman in college then. Her father was no longer in the picture, having taken up with another woman.

Sabrina was, you know, mostly over it, too.

THE THING SABRINA liked best about the high desert: the clouds. Having grown up at sea level, she was continually stunned now to see how much closer the clouds were here at seven thousand feet—how much more dramatic. This was a good day for clouds, too. A storm was coming in.

Good day for a drive? Damn straight.

She and Barry, her burly bartender boyfriend, headed north over the Rio Grande, stopping first to take pictures from the bridge. A police car had stopped traffic for a camera crew shooting a student film. But they were allowed to stroll halfway out to watch.

The wind was blowing bitter cold, and the depth of the gorge—about 650 feet—made Sabrina dizzy when she looked down. She could see herself falling and had to fight a frightening urge to jump. It would be so easy . . .

The movie scene was short and simple: a pink Cadillac convertible carries six passengers, five talking and laughing, one silent and sad, across the bridge at high speed.

Sabrina's cell phone rang and the director cried, "Cut!"

She mouthed the word "Sorry" and took the call while walking away into the wind.

"Hi, Ruby, what's going on?"

Ruby was Sabrina's younger sister—younger by six years—and generally called when she was experiencing some sort of crisis, usually minor.

"Tom and I had a fight," Ruby said.

The camera crew let some cars go through, and prepared to shoot another take.

"Let me talk to him," Sabrina said. "I'll straighten him out."

"He's not here. He left."

Sabrina was kidding. She didn't really want to talk to Tom; it was just her way of being supportive. If Ruby got that, she didn't let on. She just wanted to vent and Sabrina let her, though it was hard to hear.

After two more shots from different angles, the movie crew packed up their equipment. Sabrina and Barry continued north, the weather getting worse, darker clouds coming down from Colorado.

At Tres Piedras they thought about turning back but decided to forge on to Brazos, Chama, Antonito. They got intermittent rain. Nothing more. The clouds were dramatic, though, and the scenery spectacular. Especially Brazos Cliffs. Reminiscent of Yosemite. This far north it was much greener as well. No more barren earth. It was all covered with grass and trees—the light green of the quaking aspens and the darker green of the fir and pine. Lush valleys, and always on the horizon the dark, brooding mountains.

The only animals they saw were cows and horses, and Barry pointed out a variety of birds—ravens, vultures, and one red-tailed hawk. Possibly a golden eagle; he wasn't sure.

She liked traveling with Barry. He was quiet, observant, open to whatever, and he didn't insist on doing all the driving like some men she knew. Her father, for one.

When they crossed into Colorado, they even saw a bit of snow on a distant peak. In Antonito, they stopped to take pictures of two horses, one black, one white. They came near when Sabrina called to them. The white one stayed back a bit, but the black one stretched his neck so far over the fence that his nose almost touched the camera.

On the way back the sky was especially fascinating, with two layers of clouds moving at different speeds. Or perhaps it was only the lower clouds that were moving while the high ones stayed put and the car moved beneath them. Neither one of them had ever seen anything like it.

She did catch herself thinking, for just a moment, that it would be more fun to be doing this in Wheeler's Thunderbird with the top down for a clear view of the sky, but then she realized they could have taken Barry's Jeep Wrangler and had the same unobstructed view. She had been the one who wanted to take her car—a laser blue Mini with a white roof—because she loved driving it. But the tiny two-door hardtop didn't even have a sun roof.

IN BED THAT night Joshua tossed and turned for hours, finally falling into a fitful, feverish sleep, his sweat soaking the sheets and accentuating the sticky feeling of his dream.

He walks along the edge of a small gorge near his house. Behind him somewhere kids are laughing as they slide down the embankment in cardboard boxes that glide easily over the tall dry grass. He used to do that when he was a kid.

Ronni is with him as they stroll along the ridge out of sight of the children and away from all the houses. The heat is almost too much for him, but then they reach the trees. Then there is intermittent relief as they go in and out of the shade.

The swimsuit she's wearing is a turquoise two-piece that's too small for her—as if she outgrew it the year before but is still making do. Oddly, Joshua wears a three-piece suit. He has no idea why. As they walk, he loosens his tie, slings the jacket over his shoulder, and unbuttons his vest. He even kicks off his stiff leather shoes, peels off his sweaty socks—Woo! they smell like ammonia or worse.

He and Ronni continue down the path barefoot. Still, it's not enough. He feels sticky and uncomfortable.

Most of the hike is still ahead of them, and they are getting nowhere, although Ronni doesn't seem to mind. She simply gazes into the gorge, watching the tiny stream along the bottom that should have dried up by now. It usually only runs in winter.

Joshua, meanwhile, stashes his shoes, jacket, vest, and tie behind a tree. He throws off his shirt as well and is ready to continue the hike when Ronni comes over, opens his pants and pulls them down so he can step out of them.

Hand-in-hand, they continue down the trail, Ronni in her too-small swimsuit, Joshua in white cotton boxers. He moves more freely and feels much better. The view, he suddenly notices, is breathtaking—the gorge having become an enormous canyon.

As they walk farther and the trail dips to the bottom, Joshua feels the heat of the sun and the way his sweat-stained boxers cling to his thighs as he moves.

Ronni stops him, peels off his boxers, and leaves them on the trail. Taking his hand, she leads him farther—without stopping for a drink of the cool water in the stream. Joshua walks gingerly a half step behind. Ronni seems to forget he's there.

Finally, the trail takes them back to the top of the ridge. There they run into Dana Tierney—skinny, sunburned, and blonder than ever. She is wearing, of all things, a navy blue choir robe. It floats in a gentle breeze Joshua hadn't felt below.

Ronni says, "Oh, you know Joshua, don't you?"

Ronni has apparently forgotten all about Joshua being naked, but it doesn't escape Dana's attention.

"I'd like to," she says.

When Joshua woke up, the covers were off the bed. He was lying on his back and it was hard to go back to sleep.

8

JOSHUA TRIED TO call Ronni, who never seemed to be at home all of a sudden. Her little brother answered.

"She's baby-sitting at the Thompsons'," he said. "You should go over there."

"Why do you say that?"

"I don't know. She's probably writing a love poem to you right now."

Joshua flashed back on something Ronni had written to him months earlier, composed when she was far away, traveling with her family.

"Right. Thanks," he said.

The Thompsons' two-story adobe was in Joshua's neighborhood, so he walked over to pay her a visit. As he came up the long dirt driveway, he could see her through the small squares of the big window. The only light came from a huge flat-screen TV—explosions of light, actually, from an old war movie.

He knocked gently and she let him in but didn't seem all that happy to see him. She gave all her attention to the movie.

"Kids in bed?"

"Uh-huh."

"When do you expect . . . "

"Midnight or so."

It was now about nine-thirty.

Though Ronni was leaning forward, elbows on her knees, Joshua tried to kiss her. She leaned out of reach, eyes never leaving the TV. Joshua leaned a little farther and lost his balance. They both tumbled to the floor.

He wanted to laugh. They both should be laughing now, he thought. But he didn't feel like laughing. Ronni wasn't laughing, and she wasn't saying anything.

The carpet was thick and soft and he didn't want to get up but he did. On the TV, men were shouting at each other but not loud enough to wake the children who were sleeping somewhere in the adjoining rooms. Someone was wounded and called out for a medic. Another bomb exploded quietly.

Joshua looked at Ronni, who was still on the floor but propped up on her elbows now, looking back at him, without the slightest trace of any expression whatsoever on her face.

Whatsoever.

Joshua turned and walked out the front door.

She didn't try to stop him.

He thought to himself, I have no idea what just happened. But he did know. It was just that, in the basement of his brain, he had switched off the light, closed the door and bolted it, refusing to acknowledge what was down there. Even though he knew.

It was over between them. Not officially. Not yet. But soon.

Still, he hoped he was wrong. He could definitely be wrong. He was wrong about a lot of things. Why not this?

As he neared the end of the driveway, he looked over his shoulder and saw her standing in the window watching him go. He wondered if she could even see him now.

RATHER THAN GO out, Sabrina had invited Barry to her place for a late dinner, since he wasn't tending bar that night. She had him cutting the corn from four cobs while she chopped zucchini, onions, and fresh chiles, the cookbook from her favorite restaurant propped open on the counter of her small kitchen.

"Perdón," she said.

Barry was like this huge immovable object, but he gave way gently to Sabrina, the irresistible force, always touching her softly as she moved around.

She set two New York steaks to sizzling atop the gas range. He picked up the hickory salt and looked at her; she nodded and he sprinkled some on the steaks.

"More?"

She shook her head.

"Too much?"

"No," she said. "Just right."

She got up on her toes and kissed him quickly, but not too quickly.

The mushrooms were done, so she put them in the oven, sauté pan and all, to keep warm.

Barry refilled her glass with sangria, then topped up his own.

"Here's to you," he said. "The finest piece of ass in all of New Mexico."

"Not all the world?"

"I'll have to look into that and get back to you," he said.

She punched him in the arm and made him spill his drink all over his white linen shirt.

IT WAS MIDNIGHT and the only light in Joshua's room came from the streetlight across the street. He got up and switched on his iPad and searched his Facebook Inbox until he found the message he was looking for, next to a tiny picture of Ronni, which threw him a little because it wasn't the same picture as when she sent it, not two months earlier:

RONNI SEGER APRIL 14 AT 11:31PM

i keep thinking of something you said friday nite & it bothers me some. when you said, "you haven't kissed me like that for a long time" i thought you knew why. after that one time i really don't trust myself—i get worked up pretty easily, you know. maybe it doesn't affect you at all but i can hardly stand it when you arouse me & then we can't do anything about it. it's not fair to you, or me. we've got to be realistic we are human & we can make mistakes. that's all I can write tonite cuz i'm falling asleep fast.

I LOVE YOU, JOSHUA. DON'T EVER FORGET THAT!

*whether or not i show you every day how much i love you, i
do! it just takes me a little while to show my feelings on some
things, especially those that are personal. you know that some-
day we want to be married and then i'll try to show you my
feelings for you and how much i care but you're going to have
to give me some coaching on how i can show you best and
what i can do for you.*

all my love to you,
ronni

SABRINA HAD REMOVED Barry's sangria-stained shirt and told
him he would have to eat without it. Then she'd noticed wine
on his jeans and told him he would have to do without those,
too. He was, in fact, naked all through dinner while she re-
mained fully clothed.

After he had cleared the table, she said she wanted to watch
a movie, so they sat together on her leather sofa for two hours
while Jason Bourne tried to learn his identity.

Finally, Barry scooped her up in his arms and carried her into the bedroom. She was not a small woman—five feet nine
inches tall and solidly built—but he made her feel insubstantial
as a falling leaf—a leaf landing lightly on the bed.

Barry, still naked and still hard after more than two hours,
would last just a few minutes more.

JOSHUA CAUGHT UP with Ronni in the town square early Thursday evening as a local Los Lobos tribute band was taking the stage. She had a friend with her, Cheryl Powell, a strawberry blonde with a short body and a long face. Joshua knew her from being on the student newspaper together. They all listened for a while, then wandered around the square—Cheryl in the middle. If Joshua maneuvered around to Ronni's side, Ronni reshuffled the deck.

Later, Cheryl said, "Ronni told me she wants to cool it for a while."

"I kind of got that impression."

"I just thought I should say something."

"Yeah, I got it. Thanks. I'm slow, but I got it."

He got it; he just didn't understand it.

JOSHUA WOKE UP in darkness, feeling as if he'd just downed a cup of strong coffee—not how you want to feel in the wee hours when your body craves sleep, more sleep, *por favor.*

He refused to look at the clock on his night table, refused to even open his eyes, hoping he could drift off again. He tried to bore himself to sleep by counting every breath he took—one, two, three, four, five, six—but it wasn't working. He kept finding himself barreling down the road toward his first speeding ticket.

One, two, three, four . . .

Way up ahead, a cop car went by on a cross street. Then it backed up and stopped right in the middle of the intersection.

Joshua took his foot off the accelerator. No doubt there was a radar gun aimed right at him.

He started over. One, two, three, four, five . . .

The cop car pulled ahead. Joshua should have turned down a side street then and disappeared into the night. But he kept going. He could see now that the cop had turned his car around and was just waiting for him, feeling clever and self-righteous, to be sure.

One, two, three, four . . .

It was months ago. He had gone to traffic court. He had paid the fine. It was all behind him. It was after midnight. He was on his way home from Ronni's, the taste of her Kissy Fit lipstick still on his lips.

One, two, three . . .

Once again he is barreling down the road, going twice as fast as the legal limit. This time he turns down a side street and speeds away.

One, two . . .

He speeds away on a side street, but somehow the cop catches up to him. That's worse.

One, two, three . . .

He turns down a side street, parks in someone's driveway, shuts off the motor, and lies down.

One, two, three, four . . .

He can't sleep.

One, two . . .

He's barreling down the road.

One . . .

Ronni's lipstick.

One . . .

He tries to outrun the cop, loses control, smashes into a telephone pole.

He's bleeding but still conscious.

He still can't sleep.

9

SABRINA MET JOSHUA outside the Kit Carson House and Museum.

"Ready?" she asked

Joshua shrugged, looked terminally bored.

"Don't be that way," Sabrina said. "You said you'd be happy to go with me."

"Sorry," he said and did his best to look happy, though Sabrina wasn't fooled.

"I know it's not cool, but I haven't seen all the tourist stuff yet."

"No, it's cool," he said. "I haven't seen it either."

"You're kidding me, you've lived in this tumbleweed heaven all your life and you've never been inside the Kit Carson house?"

The boy looked at her sideways.

"Tumbleweed heaven?"

"Sure. Don't you think?"

"I wouldn't let the Visitors Bureau hear you say that."

She nudged him in the ribs.

"You the guardian of the tourist trade now?"

"Can't have people thinking we live in an imperfect paradise."

Sabrina smiled. Even on a bad day, the kid was sharp.

"Yeah," she said, "maybe that's better left unsaid."

"Anyway, who says I've lived here all my life?"

"Haven't you?"

"No," he said. "I thought you had."

"Nope."

"Well, you look like you belong here."

"Gracias. So, where are you from?"

"California."

"No kidding? Me, too," she said. "Not originally, but most recently."

"We moved here sixteen years ago."

Sabrina laughed, and Joshua looked a little happier, at least for a moment.

"Then I'm still the new kid on the block."

She bought tickets and they went inside to look at all the old photos, maps, guns, knives, clothing, low doorways, short beds, and other artifacts.

"Where did you live in California?" Joshua asked.

"I moved to L.A. when I was twenty-three."

"Why L.A.?"

"The usual reason. I wanted to be a movie star."

"I thought so. You look the part."

Sabrina tousled his hair.

"I was not the prettiest girl in town, believe me."

"It's not all about looks, though, is it?"

"Pretty is just table stakes. That, and talent. Then you need to be lucky."

"You weren't?"

Sabrina shook her head. Her experience of Hollywood? The place was full of men eager to tell you what they could do for you. Which seemed quite alright when the man in question was handsome, rich, and charming. Unfortunately most were not. Most were old, fat, and had way too many bad habits. It was all about what they wanted to do to you rather than for you. Either way, though, it was hard to feel good about yourself. Easy to lose your way.

"Look at this," she said.

There was an old map on the wall, detailed in some areas, blank in others.

Joshua looked but didn't see until Sabrina explained.

"All the blank spaces represent unexplored territory," she said.

The map noted that those areas were thought to contain "savage tribes, which no traveler has yet seen or described."

LATER, JOSHUA WENT into town just to hang out and kill time. Ronni was there. She led him into a quiet courtyard, near a shop that was temporarily closed, a sign in the door showing the time when the owner would return.

"I know you're unhappy, but please try not to be," she said. "I know I hurt you. I'm sorry. I am. But you know this is better."

"It doesn't feel better," Joshua said.

"We're too young to get serious with anyone."

He looked down at the cracked cement beneath his tennis shoes, shook his head, fought back tears.

"But I am serious," he said.

"Look," she said, "this is hard for me, too."

"I thought you were seri—"

The word caught in Joshua's throat. He could see her message on his computer screen—*You know some day we want to be married*—and he remembered how it made him feel, and now he was crying and trying to hide it and not having much success.

Ronni seemed a little exasperated, though she was doing a stellar job of containing it. He would give her that.

"I have to let go," she said, "and so do you."

Joshua wiped his face as fast as he could, looked at the sky, and blinked rapidly. Ronni's phone buzzed twice. She looked at it and put it away.

"What? What was that?"

"Nothing. Doesn't matter," she said. "Look, I want you to understand, but I can tell you don't."

Joshua looked at his feet again and said nothing. Finally, Ronni continued.

"I'm trying, and working on myself isn't easy," she said, "but maybe I'm not the only one who needs to work out a few things."

The whole town seemed silent now except for the soft sound made by a breeze passing through a brass wind chime in the courtyard. He didn't know what he needed to work out.

"I'll grow this summer and so will you. I don't know what's going to happen in the future and I don't want to know. Just, please, try to understand."

The shopkeeper returned and was unlocking the door.

Ronni said, "Look at this as a chance to get to know lots more people."

SABRINA TURNED ON the CD player in her bedroom, turned it up loud. This was her favorite room. She loved how the textured orange walls looked ancient, thanks to a rag-on painting technique she used. She loved the old pine dresser. Loved the wrought iron bed with the just-right mattress. Loved the down comforter, the oversized pillows, and the buttery 300-thread-count sheets.

Opening her lingerie drawer, she selected a favorite bra— black with blue trim—that she had first seen in a shop window in Rome. There was something about the window displays all over the city. They were provocative yet tasteful, elegant. This one, she remembered, had stopped her in her tracks. Inside, an older woman helped her find what she was looking for.

"Your size?" she had asked.

Before Sabrina could answer—she knew sizes were different in Italy—the woman had cupped her right breast and bounced it lightly in her palm.

Then, when she tried what the woman gave her, it fit perfectly.

"Bellissimo!" the woman cried when she came to check on Sabrina.

Yes, Bellissimo, Sabrina thought. She realized the woman wanted to make a sale, but there was such delight in her voice.

"Bellissimo!" Sabrina said to herself now as she hooked the clasps behind her back. She stepped into the matching thong, turned her back to the mirror, and looked over her shoulder. Bellissimo, indeed.

Sabrina's companion at the time was a Hollywood agent— Roger Burnett of Burnett & Associates—who entertained clients at the restaurant where she had been waiting tables, hoping to somehow break into films like so many other aspiring actresses. He paid for everything—panties, bras, garter belts, stockings, a waist cincher she hardly needed but loved for the way it held her tight.

Most of her believed he was in love with her. Maybe he was then. It didn't matter now.

Now she zipped herself into a little black dress and turned from side to side, letting the short hem dance against her thighs. Then, impulsively, she knelt on her bed and leaned forward on her elbows. A gentle breeze came through the open window and her sheer white curtains had their turn to dance.

If anyone came into the room right now, she promised herself she wouldn't turn around. She wouldn't move. Not that anyone would just walk into her house, even if the doors were unlocked. Not that they would just crawl in through an open window. But if they did.

JOSHUA SAT ON the ground under Sabrina's window hugging his knees and hurting inside.

Through the window he could hear her stereo and the music was beautiful but sad. Or he thought it was sad. Just now a marching band would sound sad.

He hugged his knees tighter and listened.

What he heard most clearly was a piano, and he imagined the slow careful dance of fingers across the keys. Careful. Careful. The keys might break. Then he heard an angelic voice forming words in a language he didn't know, or maybe they weren't words at all but just feelings nobody could describe. Then came the thunder of what had to be humongous drums. A storm raging.

As far as he could tell the pain was never going to stop.

BETWEEN TRACKS, SABRINA heard an odd noise and went to look out the window.

"Joshua?"

He didn't respond.

"Joshua!"

She ducked back inside to turn down the music and this time heard a distinct thud.

"Are you okay?"

The boy was doubled over, holding his head and bobbing up and down like an oil derrick. He must have hit his head on the edge of her rollout window when he got up.

"Come inside," she said.

When she opened the front door, he was wiping his face with his hands.

"What were you doing under my bedroom window?" she asked.

"Listening," he said.

She put her hands on her hips and stared at him, her eyes narrowing.

"To the music," he added. "I was listening to the music."

Sabrina let him in and shut the door.

"You can't just camp out under a woman's bedroom window," she said. "That is not okay."

"Sorry," he said. "I'm really sorry."

"Never mind that now. Sit down. How's your head?"

He shrugged, sniffed, ran his hand over his face again. She sat beside him on the sofa.

"Have you been crying?"

The boy looked at his shoes; she touched his head gently and brushed back his hair. This could only be one thing.

"Do you want me to break her knee caps for you?" she asked.

He sort of laughed and looked up at her.

"That won't be necessary," he said.

"I will, you know. Just say the word."

"Thanks," he said. "Let me think about it."

Sabrina brushed his hair again with her fingers.

"You need a part," she said.

"What, like in a play?"

She smiled.

"Here, let me get a comb."

From the end table, she picked up her purse, found her turquoise comb, and dragged it over his head. He flinched; she winced.

"Sorry," she said. "I'll avoid that spot."

She carefully combed his two-tone hair forward until it was all in his face, which is where is was most of the time anyway.

"Do you know how to find your natural part?" she asked.

Joshua shook his head.

"I'll show you."

From the spiral pattern on the back of his head, she drew a line straight forward and parted his hair on either side of it.

"There," she said. "That's better. I can see your forehead now."

He shrugged.

"Come with me."

Sabrina lead him into the bathroom and stood him in front of the mirror.

"What do you think?"

"I like it," he said, "but it's not going to stay like that."

"I have just the thing. Close your eyes."

She sprayed his hair with Freeze and Shine Super Spray, a hurricane-strength product from the Hair Today salon where she worked.

"If this doesn't hold it, nothing will," she said.

He opened his eyes and they smiled at each other in the mirror. Instead of a goofy mop-topped kid Sabrina saw a serious if somewhat red-eyed young man.

"Better?" she asked.

He nodded.

TARA ARRIVED IN time to see the boy pedal away from Sabrina's house on his bike. She was wearing a stretchy scoop-neck top that showed off her chest. Which was typical for the never-shy redhead.

"Who was that?" she wanted to know.

"Joshua."

"And he is?"

"The boy who broke my window."

"He's cute. Have you gotten into his pants yet?"

"He's seventeen, Tara."

"So?"

"So it's out of the question."

"Not for me it isn't."

Sabrina shook her head, stared Tara down.

"What?"

"He's a good kid, Tara. You fuck with him, you'll have me to answer to."

"Fine. Just don't act like you haven't thought about it."

10

IT WAS SATURDAY night at the Shadow Dance Bar & Grill, a small, crowded, dimly lit place with the bleached skull and long horns of a once-proud steer looking down from the exposed rafters, a string of electric chiles glowing red behind the bar. Sabrina was the designated driver, so Tara was feeling free to toss back as many shots as she wanted. Which was a lot, from the look of things.

Sabrina sat next to her at the thickly varnished bar, sipping a single margarita—on the rocks, with salt, keep the silly straw, thank you very much—and avoiding eye contact with a young cowboy who always seemed to be looking her way.

Sure enough, he was already too drunk to take a hint and asked her to dance.

"She's taken," Tara said, "but I'll dance with you."

The cowboy looked at Sabrina, Sabrina turned away.

Barry, in a crisp white shirt and bolo tie, was tending bar as usual. He asked Sabrina if she wanted another.

"I do," she said.

"Yeah?"

She smiled. They both knew she couldn't hold her liquor. She was already lightheaded.

Sabrina watched Tara dance with the cowboy—or rather for the cowboy—who now had eyes only for her. It was quite a performance, and Sabrina knew from other such Saturdays that it would only get better . . .

JOSHUA HAD A part-time job busing tables at a popular tacqueria overlooking the town square. He mostly worked the lunch shift, like today, but sometimes the night shift and sometimes both, since the other busboys weren't too reliable.

The place was painted five different colors, each of them pretty extreme, and there were hundreds of figures, most of them stars, hanging from the ceilings. On the outdoor patio, Joshua was clearing a four-top when he noticed one of the last people he wanted to see just then, Cheryl. The girl with the short body and long face. The girl who seemed to enjoy telling him Ronni wanted to cool it. She and a girlfriend were being seated by the railing. Cheryl was completely absorbed in her Blackberry, giggling and typing rapidly with her thumbs. Not to be left out, her friend started doing the same on her iPhone. With any luck, Joshua thought, they wouldn't see him, but—

"Hey, I know you," Cheryl said.

Joshua smiled self-consciously and continued gathering empty plates. Cheryl motioned him over.

"You should call Ronni," she said.

Joshua stared at her blankly.

"No, really. Call her tonight," Cheryl said. "She'll go out with you."

"She just broke up with me."

"I know, but she's having second thoughts. She told me."

"She wants me to call her?"

"Absolutely."

TARA WAS THE kind of woman who would get drunk and take her top off at parties. You couldn't really blame her, though. She did have phenomenal breasts, and people liked seeing them.

Saturday, though, was the first time Tara had yanked her top off in a bar—an exceedingly crowded bar.

It was funny but even women got horny when Tara was showing off her charms. Well, some women. Others were just annoyed. But some felt compelled to join in the girls-gone-wild fun. As if Taos were a Spring Break hot spot. Sabrina had seen it before. But she had never joined in.

Until Saturday night.

JOSHUA PUNCHED RONNI'S number. Hung up the phone. Punched the number again. Hung up. Punched fast and held his breath.

"Hi, Ronni?"

"Yes."

"This is Joshua."

"I know."

Her voice sounded flat.

"So, how are you?" he said.

"I'm fine."

Already this was not going well.

"Hey," he said, "I was wondering if you'd like to see a movie with me tonight."

"No."

"Um, well, I thought . . . "

"I know."

His father was in the next room and Joshua hoped he wasn't listening.

"You don't want to go?"

"No."

He waited. Nada. Obviously, this was as awkward for her as it was for him.

"See you," he said and hung up the phone.

SABRINA WAS PRETTY sure that—after too, too many margaritas—she had brushed nipples with Tara on the dance floor. But had she really shouted "Bellissimo! Bellissimo!" over and over? Had Wheeler been there in the flesh, or had those damn blue eyes of his only shown up in her dream later? Her recollection was hazy.

Everyone else, on the other hand, seemed to have perfect recall.

IN THE MORNING, Joshua went to the bookstore where he knew Cheryl worked. He found her down one of the narrow aisles, putting new novels on the bottom shelf. In the gap between her low-slung jeans and her two different-colored tank tops, Joshua had a nice view of her purple thong, but he composed himself.

"Thanks for the tip," he said.

Cheryl stood up.

"Oh, God, I'm sorry," she said. "She changed her mind after I talked to you."

Was she really sorry? Joshua didn't think so. This was a girl who once told Ronni: "Just do what I do. Go out with a guy once and break it off. Does wonders for your self-esteem." Ronni hadn't listened to her. Why had he?

"You could have warned me," he said.

Cheryl picked up more books from the cart next to her.

"How?" she said. "I don't have your number."

"Right. How hard would that be to find?"

11

SABRINA WAS GIVING Joshua a haircut in her kitchen when a muddy Jeep Wrangler pulled into the driveway. She couldn't actually see it from where she stood, but she recognized the sound of the engine. Had to be Barry.

He came in through the side door without knocking.

"What's going on?" he said.

He was wearing brand new work boots—the mustard-colored kind with white soles and leather laces. His blue jeans were rolled up at the ankles to form cuffs, and he had on a faded red T-shirt that fit a little too tight given the roundness of his belly, though Sabrina found it oddly endearing.

"Have a seat," Sabrina said. "I'll be done in a minute."

"Who's this then?"

"Barry, this is Joshua. You know, the boy who broke my window."

"He breaks your window and you give him a haircut. I thought he was supposed to be working for you, not the other way around."

"He's done plenty for me already, so I wanted to do this for him."

Barry shook his head, sat down at the table.

"At least in the salon you have magazines," he said.

"My boyfriend's a little impatient," Sabrina said to Joshua. (And perhaps a bit angry with her, though she didn't mention that.)

Barry drummed his fingers on the table and looked around aimlessly as Sabrina continued to fuss with Joshua's hair, snipping a little more here, a little more there.

Finally, Barry stood up.

"I'll come back later," he said and was out the door.

Joshua glanced at Sabrina.

"Nice guy," he said.

"Barry? He has his good points."

"If you go for the snarly bad-boy type."

Sabrina laughed.

"You see right through me, don't you?"

The truth was Barry was exceedingly gentle—a big teddy bear—and she sometimes wished he were more like his image.

IT WAS BARRY of course who had taken her home from the Shadow Dance. It must have been. Tara couldn't drive, let alone get Sabrina into the car. But he was not there when she woke up.

He was back now, sitting on a high stool in her kitchen, covered with an oversized beach towel, about to get his hair cut.

"You're still hung up on that son of a bitch, aren't you?" he said, looking straight ahead as Sabrina snipped away at his hair.

"Who?"

"Who! You know who."

"I'm afraid I don't."

"Yes, you do."

"Who?"

"You know. Mr. Smooth Talker. What's his name? Wheeler-dealer."

Sabrina laughed. It was funny how they both pretended not to remember each other's names.

"I'm not hung up on him, Barry. I'm hung up on you."

"Don't bullshit me, Sabrina."

NONE OF JOSHUA'S friends played tennis, not well, so Joshua would just go to the park and hit against the practice wall, hoping some other partnerless player would show up.

Today it was Tony Herrero, who he knew, sort of, from school. Nice enough guy, kind of quiet, drove a red Mustang with one black fender—a junkyard replacement part still waiting to be painted—and played reasonably well. Wicked forehand, lame backhand.

They played a couple of games, and Joshua suddenly noticed Ronni standing behind the chain-link fence, watching him, or watching them, he wasn't sure.

He remembered being here with her, trying to teach her how to play, when they were still together. It had not gone well: Every time he had casually approached the net, she would try to blast the ball past him, which rarely worked. But when it did, oh, man, he heard about it.

Now he heard her cheer as Tony won a point.

Was she dating Tony now? Really? Tony?

The two players traded sides, so now Ronni was right behind Joshua and still she cheered for Tony, though he didn't give her much to cheer about, not with the wind against him now.

At one point, Joshua stopped and just looked at her.

She shrugged with just her right shoulder.

He went to pick up a ball that had rolled up against the fence right at her feet.

"Sorry," she said. "He needs the encouragement."

BARRY COULDN'T SEEM to let go of the fact that Sabrina had entered "a titty shaking contest," as he called it, only after Wheeler had showed up at the Shadow Dance.

"I wasn't really aware of who was there," Sabrina said.

"Oh, I think you were."

"Well, I wasn't."

"Sabrina," he said, "I know what I saw."

"Well, I don't know what you saw, but I can assure you I—"

"Can you?"

She swept his hair off the kitchen floor and dumped it in the garbage under the sink.

"I can assure you I think Wheeler is a jerk and worse."

"You got that right," he muttered.

"And who's here with me now? Him? Or you?"

"Me."

She knelt down in front of him.

"And whose belt am I unbuckling right now?"

JOSHUA TOLD SABRINA about his encounter with Ronni the next day and asked her to explain it to him.

"Sometimes a girl likes to feel needed," she said.

"What should I have done? Let him win, so she could feel sorry for me?"

"What do you think?"

"I don't know what to think. That's why I'm asking you."

"What makes you think I know?"

Joshua turned up his palms, hunched his shoulders.

"Because you're really smart?" he said.

Sabrina laughed.

"Good answer," she said.

"At least I thought you were," he added.

"Listen, nobody knows what anybody else wants from them at any given moment," she said. "Could be one thing now, the opposite later."

NIGHT WAS FALLING and Joshua opened his bedroom window, turned out the light, and sat on the bed. The streetlight on the other side of the street had burned out, which gave him a better view of the darkening sky, its color changing from sad to angry to forgiving and finally, midnight black and white.

Earlier, when he was sitting on Sabrina's sofa, his hand had inadvertently slipped between the cushions. He felt something there and pulled out a skimpy bit of black lace. Sabrina was in the kitchen just then. He quickly stuffed her misplaced panties back between the cushions. Then, just before she returned to the living room, he changed his mind and slipped them into his pocket.

Which is where he found them now.

He was torn because he didn't think he should be thinking of her the way he was . . . At times his feelings for her were kind of like the feelings he had for his mother, which seemed almost disloyal. But this was different.

The really remarkable part, he supposed, was he didn't feel shy or awkward around Sabrina—at least not as shy or as awkward as he normally did around, let's face it, any attractive female. He trusted her. Right away. He could tell she had a good heart and wouldn't hurt him. He could expose himself without feeling vulnerable.

The way he was feeling now, though, was sort of, well, wicked, in the old-fashioned sense of the word. That she would want the same thing seemed highly unlikely. Then again . . .

It was all too easy to imagine the lace fabric in his hands stretched across Sabrina's hips and tucked tightly between her legs.

SABRINA WAS SITTING on the floor in her bedroom, feeling comfortable in a silk camisole and tap pants. The lights were out, the window open, the stars reaching out to her through the night sky. She checked her posture—back straight, chin down slightly, wrists resting on her knees—and took a deep breath. Then she let it all out slowly, completely, and felt her lungs refill of their own accord.

She liked that part—noticing how her lungs went about their business.

Thoughts sprang up in her mind like grass coming up in a meadow after a spring rain. That's how she thought of it, how she was trained to think of it. Completely natural. That's what the brain does; it grows thoughts. But you can let them go.

She thought about Barry and why she wanted him and yet she didn't.

She let it go.

She thought about Wheeler and why she didn't want him and yet she did.

She let it go.

She thought about Tara and how she said things Sabrina would never allow herself to even think.

She let it go.

She thought about her posture and checked it again. Her lower back was bowing out. She straightened it and breathed deeply.

She thought about the hair salon and whether she should move on—rent a chair someplace instead of working for Juanita.

She tried to let it go.

It would be a bit riskier but she'd be able to keep everything she took in, minus the rent of course. Would her regular clients follow her to a new location? Even if it were less convenient?

She let it go (for now).

She thought about painting and how she mostly loved it and sometimes hated it—how she wished she could get more of the images in her head onto paper or canvas.

She let it go.

She thought about painting a meadow in the spring when the grass is just coming up, only each blade is a brand new thought. The blades in the foreground are large enough to . . .

She let it go.

No, that was an interesting idea. She'd hang on to that.

She thought about Joshua . . . and let it go.

IF JOSHUA WAS passing by Sabrina's place and saw Barry's Jeep outside, he would just keep going. He didn't want to intrude, and Barry definitely made him feel like an intruder—even if Joshua was there first and Barry showed up later. You could almost think Barry was jealous, but that would be ridiculous.

Joshua was jealous.

Not seriously, but yeah—Barry was one lucky dude. No doubt about it.

He could be a dick sometimes, but not always. He had his redeeming qualities, or so Sabrina said. She just wanted everyone to get along.

So there was this time when he and Sabrina were in her kitchen, happily talking away—he was telling her about some of the actual headlines his journalism teacher liked to read to the class, like "Iraqi Head Seeks Arms" and "Prostitutes Appeal to Pope" and "Kids Make Nutritious Snacks"—and then Barry came in. He helped himself to a cold one and downed half the bottle in one go. Joshua said he really should be going, but Sabrina told him to relax, stay awhile.

"You know," she said, "Barry used to be a newspaperman."

"Really?"

Joshua was surprised, and he had never met a bona fide reporter. (Not counting his teacher, who probably hadn't done any real reporting in at least a decade.)

"Oh, gawwwd," Barry said, "what'd you have to bring that up for?"

"Maybe you could give Joshua some advice—he's a budding reporter."

Barry finished his Pacifico and set the bottle down on the counter. He looked at Sabrina for what felt like a long while, then turned to Joshua.

"Fine," he said. "My advice to you, young man, is find something else to do."

"Why?"

"You know, for a budding reporter you're sadly uninformed. Newspapers are dead, man. Dead or dying. They didn't tell you that at school?"

For once, Joshua didn't let Barry's asshole routine deter him.

"What paper did you write for?" he asked.

"Doesn't matter," Barry said. "Doesn't exist. Not anymore."

"But there are still lots of papers out there, right?"

Barry went to the fridge and grabbed another tall brown bottle, popped the top with an opener clinging to the side of the old ice box with a magnetic grip, his hand landing on it as if on autopilot.

"All I can tell you is I worked for three papers in three states, dude, and they are gone, gone, and, let me see . . . gone."

"That sucks."

"Tell me about it."

Barry took a drink and stared out the kitchen window.

Sabrina said, "Lighten up, would you, Barry?"

He didn't answer, just kept staring out the window.

"What about the Internet?" Joshua said. "Online journalism? Yahoo hired this guy to go around the world and report from all the war zones."

The light changed as a cloud moved to block the sun. Barry suddenly stirred.

"That what you want to do?" he asked. "You want to be Kevin Sites."

"No."

"Yeah, me neither."

TWO DAYS LATER, Barry came to the tacqueria with a buddy and stopped Joshua to say he was sorry for acting like a jerk.

"No worries," Joshua said.

"The truth is I was never what you'd call a savvy reporter. People would lie to me and I would believe them," he said. "Ask this guy here."

Barry's friend just smiled and shook his head, looked down at his menu.

"I got used and I got fired and I never learned," Barry said.

"That sucks."

"Yeah, sucks to be me, huh?"

"No, I—"

Joshua didn't know what to say.

"Relax, man, I was kidding. It doesn't suck at all. Life is good. I'm happy. Do what makes you happy."

"Thanks. I will. I'll try."

Barry smiled then, and for the first time Joshua kind of liked him. At least he wasn't a complete ass.

"There is no try, only do," Barry said, and then he laughed. "Sorry. Didn't mean to get all mystical on you."

Joshua said, "Isn't that from, like, *Star Wars* or something?"

Barry paused for a second and slowly smiled.

"Yeah," he said. "I guess it is."

SOMEHOW JOSHUA FOUND himself in a debate about which sport was the most physically demanding.

A few of his sometimes friends from the paper where clustered in the town square, and Bradford—puffing on a cigar just as he had been the last time Joshua had seen him—called him over to ask what he thought.

"Joshua, Joshua! Hey, man, give us the benefit of your considered opinion."

Joshua took off his sunglasses and started cleaning the lenses with the tail of his shirt. Bradford grew impatient.

"Soccer rules! Am I right?"

Joshua put his sunglasses back on, shook his head.

"Mmm, I'd have to say basketball."

"Dude! No way."

Now the debate was back on, with others in the group saying football was the toughest. No, wrestling. No, gymnastics.

Ronni, who was the only girl in the group, seemed to be with Bradford now, which surprised Joshua, again. Apparently she had meant what she said about getting to know lots of people.

"What about boxing?" she said. "Those boys really take a pounding."

Wearing a striped top and snug-fitting capri pants, Ronni looked painfully beautiful to him just then. Heart-attack beautiful.

"What do you know about it?" Joshua said. "You couldn't punch your way out of a soap bubble?"

"Oh, yeah? Come on, tough guy, I'll take you on."

Joshua tried to ignore her but she started bouncing around on her toes, waving her hands in his face, taunting him like some pesky fly.

He flinched.

"Ah-ha!"

Ronni's open palms whizzed past his face, closer each time. He backpedaled to keep his balance.

"Hey, come on . . . "

She kept shuffling around him.

"What's the matter?" she said. "You afraid of me?"

Slap boxing was a playground game that started as friendly sparring, but then each fighter would try to show he could win if it were for real. Which Joshua really didn't want to happen now, in the middle of the town square, but Ronni kept up her taunts.

"A soap bubble, huh? Better watch out. I'll slap you silly."

Joshua felt a rush of air by his ear as he dodged Ronni's flashing right, moved away, and hitched up his jeans, which suddenly felt baggy and cumbersome. He took a couple of tentative swipes at her, not really wanting to connect. He'd be an ass if he did.

Why doesn't she just stop? he thought. I'll stop if she does.

There was a new kid there, someone's cousin from out of town, who shouted, "Come on, Ronnie, you going to let her jerk you around like that?"

Joshua looked at the guy like he was nuts.

"She's Ronni," he corrected.

Then he felt the slap and heard the hoots that erupted from ringside.

Bradford grabbed Ronni's hand, lifted it high above her head, and proclaimed, "The winner and still champion . . . "

Wide-eyed, Ronni clamped her other hand over her mouth.

"Are you alright?" she asked.

Joshua rubbed his cheek.

"Boxing. Yes. Definitely the toughest," he said.

LATER, AT HOME, he would remember this:

His father is talking to their pastor, who mentions how odd it is that the Bible tells husbands to love their wives but only tells wives to submit to their husbands. His father disagrees and is later proved right. Wives *are* instructed to love their husbands.

For some reason—he can't remember how it came up—Joshua relays the story to Ronni as they're walking away from the church.

"Now," she says, "if they could just find a verse that tells husbands to submit to their wives."

She smiles and bumps his shoulder, knocking him off balance.

The truth: She looks so unbelievable just then, with that smile and the twinkle in her eyes, that he knows he would submit to her gladly, no questions asked, no matter what the Bible said.

He also remembered this:

He and Ronni are playing tennis. She's receiving his serve and he's really going easy on her because she's just a beginner. But she gets bored and starts clowning around, acting like she's the catcher in a baseball game.

"Come on, now," she says. "Hum 'er in there, old boy."

She sounds like her father.

Joshua tosses the ball up high, coils, springs, and smacks it like never before.

Ronni ducks, racket shielding her head, and the ball whizzes past her ear on its way to the back fence, where it sets the chain links rattling.

"Hey!"

"Sorry," he says.

12

JOSHUA CAME AROUND the corner driving a little too fast, and there was Sabrina, dressed for work in a silk shirt and denim skirt. She was just unlocking her car, and she swiveled to see who was coming so fast so early in the morning. He waved but the sun must have been in her eyes. She didn't recognize him until he parked his shiny black MG Midget right beside her.

"New car?" she said.

"New to me. What do you think?"

His father, acting as both banker and chief negotiator, had helped him buy it the night before from a young mechanic who didn't want to part with it but was starting a family and needed a bigger car.

Sabrina looked it over, said, "Nice."

"I should really impress the girls in this."

Joshua had meant to be sardonic—a new favorite word to go along with insouciant, quintessential, juxtaposed, and all the others he collected—but he sounded almost cheerful, he thought, and that surprised him.

Sabrina smiled.

"Definitely," she said.

"Girls aren't really impressed by cars, are they?"

"Mmmm, it doesn't hurt."

"Really?"

Joshua was surprised, disappointed, and oddly pleased—after all, he had the car now.

"Well, the guy has to look at least as good as the car," Sabrina said.

"That counts me out."

"No, it doesn't."

"No?"

"I think you're quite handsome."

"That's a first."

"Why do you say that?"

"No one's ever called me handsome before."

"No—really?"

"Never."

"Maybe that's because they didn't want to state the obvious."

"Now you're laying it on a bit thick."

"Well, I think you're good-looking."

"I see, now I'm just good-looking. What's next: 'not too ugly'?"

"Okay, let's just say I wouldn't be ashamed to be seen with you in public."

Joshua laughed. Flirting with Sabrina was fun—if pointless—and he felt sort of, well, happy, for the first time in too long. Not that he expected it to last.

"Now we're getting down to it," he said. "Alright then, where are we going tonight?"

"You want to have dinner?"

"Um, sure."

"Pick me up at eight."

THEY WENT TO a place she said she liked in town and were seated in the courtyard, a pleasant spot with a fountain and two trees (one of them with apples). Large white umbrellas and green umbrellas adorned the many small tables. A folk duo—guitar and bass—serenaded everyone as the sun went down and candles glowed.

Halfway through their entrees, Sabrina leaned close, touched Joshua's hand, and whispered, "Don't look now, but I think this girl in the corner wants you."

He started to turn his head, but she caught his chin.

"Uh-uh," she said.

She looked into his eyes and he smiled, holding her gaze. To anyone watching it would look like they couldn't take their eyes off each other.

"What is it about the words don't look now that confuses people?" she said.

He laughed and so did she.

Later, he noticed a girl watching him as she cleared empty plates from a nearby table. She quickly lowered her eyes and walked away.

He had a feeling he had seen her before but he couldn't remember where.

WITH A BUCKET of old tennis balls, Joshua headed down to the park and started hitting serves. He hit one neatly down the middle and heard some guy say, "Not bad."

"Thanks," he said.

"Can I give you a tip?"

"Sure."

The man was tall and lean, his long black hair held back by a blue bandana, his beard neatly trimmed.

"It's your toss," he said. "It's a little too far out to the side. Gives you a sort of looping swing. You want to try to place the ball a little higher and a little more . . . Here, let me show you."

The man snapped a serve down the middle, easily twice as fast as Joshua had.

"You want your arm fully extended and then . . . "

He served another, perfectly, springing forward and throwing his whole body into a fluid follow-through.

"Easy for you," Joshua said.

"Hey, listen, do I know you?"

"I don't think so."

The man tugged his shirt where it had bunched up around his right shoulder and let the fabric resettle.

"No, yeah," he said, "I've seen you somewhere."

Joshua shook his head slowly.

"Yeah, yeah, we have a mutual friend. I saw you with her. Sabrina Carlsen."

"How do you know Sabrina?"

"We used to go out, you know, before."

"Before what?"

"Before you guys hooked up."

"Oh, uh . . . "

"You're lucky, kid. She is one helluva woman. Am I right?"

"Yeah, she is. She's hot, really hot."

A GUY WALKED into the salon, and when Sabrina looked up she thought he looked vaguely familiar. He looked at her, looked again like maybe he recognized her, and then waved. She smiled and went back to coloring her client's hair.

"I need a trim," he said.

The owner, a rotund older woman named Juanita Torres, was at the counter and said, "I can take you right now."

"No," he said. "I want her. I want her to do it."

Sabrina looked up, tried to figure out how she might know him. It was surprising how many people wandered into the salon who knew her or thought they knew her.

"I'll be a while," she said.

"I'll wait."

He took a chair, picked up a magazine. Sabrina decided she didn't know him, had probably just seen him around somewhere, Taos being a small town. She caught him looking at her several times.

"You're up," she said finally.

He bounded up, grinning, and he kept grinning as she wrapped him in her vinyl cape, led him to the row of sinks at the back of the salon, washed his hair, and sat him back in her chair.

"So," she said. "A trim?"

"Trim, yes."

"A little off the sides?"

He nodded.

"The top, too?"

"Take off as much as you like," he said.

"As much as I like?"

"You like to take it off, don't you?"

"It's what I do," she said, confused.

"I'll tell you what," he said. "I'll pay you double if you take off your top."

"Excuse me?"

"Ever since I saw you dance the other night . . . "

She untied the cape, ripped it away.

"Get out," she said.

"Hey, hey, relax. I'm just saying, I . . . "

"Out!"

SABRINA WAS IN her front yard painting the sky when Tara showed up and, first thing, said: "You little liar."

The sky was changing and Sabrina didn't want to miss it.

"What?" she said.

It was perfect now and she tried to match its brilliance with quick strokes of color.

"He's a good kid, you said. Don't fuck with him, you said."

Sabrina glanced at Tara, perplexed.

"Joshua?"

"Who else?"

"He is a good kid," Sabrina said.

"Yeah, good in bed, eh?"

The light changed and Sabrina stopped painting.

"What? You think I'm sleeping with him?"

"I have to say, you had me fooled."

Sabrina closed her eyes and tried to burn the setting sun into her memory.

"Why would you think that?"

"Oh, come on, Sabrina."

"Who have you been talking to?"

"Nice try. Just give it up."

"Who, Tara?"

"Doesn't matter."

Sabrina started to gather her things.

"It does to me," she said.

"Sabrina, it's all over town."

ON THE CORNER of Paseo del Pueblo and Kit Carson Avenue, Joshua coasted up to the light and shifted into first. He found that he had to rev the engine to keep it from dying, but only on blistering days like today. Something about the design of the MG's carburetor.

A familiar voice yelled, "Sweet ride!"

On the sidewalk were Ronni and her friend Cheryl.

"Thanks," he said.

They came closer, looking the car over. He had just given it a fresh coat of wax and you could see yourself in the shine.

Ronni surprised him by asking if she could drive it sometime.

"Think you can handle a stick?" he asked.

"Why not?"

"I don't know," he said. "You might wreck it."

She put her hands on her hips, and although she was smiling, it pained him to see her like that. He didn't know why. His engine died and he tried to get it started again.

To Ronni, but loud enough for Joshua to hear, Cheryl said, "Looks like it's already a wreck."

The light changed. He tried again. The car behind him honked. He turned the key once more, stepped on the gas, and . . . yes! He let out the clutch and burned rubber through the intersection.

He felt like an ass.

WHEELER CAME INTO the salon for a haircut. Which was fine. His hair was easy to cut and he tipped well. Sabrina was pretty sure he wouldn't ask her to work topless.

"I understand there's a new man in your life," he said.

She led him over to the sink to wash his hair.

"You mean Barry?"

"Is that his name?"

She ran warm water through his hair and added a dollop of shampoo, which she worked into a rich lather.

"Wheeler," she said, just a tiniest bit of exasperation coming into her voice, "I've been seeing him for six months."

He always enjoyed this part, she could tell, and she took her time massaging his scalp.

"No, right. I know. Not Barry. The other one. The young kid."

THE NEXT DAY, when Joshua showed up ready to tend the garden or just hang out, Sabrina confronted him.

"Any idea why Wheeler would think I'm sleeping with you?"

"Who's Wheeler?"

"My old boyfriend. Plays tennis."

"Oh."

"Ring a bell for you now, does it?"

"I met a guy on the courts who said he knows you."

"But you have no idea why he would say—let's see, how did he put it?—that I'm fucking your little brains out?"

"I didn't tell him that."

"No?"

Sabrina put her hands on her hips and waited for the boy to answer.

"I mean, he may have thought that . . . "

"Uh-huh."

"But he thought that before I met him."

"I see. And you just let him continue to assume that I make a habit of molesting underage boys."

"No, I just . . . I thought . . . "

"You thought what exactly?"

"I thought it might be good for you if—"

"Good for me! This is not good for me, Joshua."

"I mean good if, if, well . . . he seemed jealous."

"You didn't think about . . . oh, for godsake."

"What?"

"Joshua, you're seventeen. If I slept with you it would be rape. Statutory rape. Now everyone thinks . . . "

"I'm sorry, Sabrina. I didn't . . . I was just . . . I don't know. I guess I was flattered he would think, you know, what he thought."

She sighed.

"Go home, Joshua."

"I'm really sorry."

"Just go home please."

13

EARLY IN THE morning, Joshua drove to Bandelier, parked the MG, and followed a paved trail back into the canyon. On his left the Frijoles River was little more than a trickle, but the cottonwood trees grew tall on its banks. Continuing on a dirt path, he passed through the remains of a circular pueblo and continued to the steep cliffs to see what was left of the Long House.

The smoke from fires that burned 800 years earlier still blackened many of the hand-carved caves. There were holes in the cliff that once held the roof beams of dwellings that were two and three stories high, and he could see carvings, petroglyphs, etched above the former rooftops.

Further up the canyon, on the other side of the stream, he came to a series of four ladders that led up to an ancient ceremonial kiva.

"Yo, Joshua! *Que pasa?*"

It was Bradford, and with him was Jason Castellini, who everyone knew because he was the tallest kid in their school, a three-sport letterman who stood about six-foot-four. They had just come down the last ladder.

"So how is it up there?"

"It's cool," Bradford said.

"Worth the climb?"

"Totally. Totally worth it. So, uh, I hear you've been banging that hairstylist—what's her name?"

"Lucky bastard," Jason chimed in.

"I'm not banging anyone."

"Right. Sorry, didn't mean to be crude," Bradford said. "Sleeping with her, then."

"Making love. That what you call it?" Jason said.

Joshua looked him in the eye and shook his head.

"I don't call it anything," he said.

"But she's a demon in the sack, right?"

"I wouldn't know."

"Come on, dude, how can you not share details with us," Bradford said. "Inquiring minds want to know."

"Forget it. Joshua's a gentleman."

The way Jason said gentleman didn't sound like a compliment.

"Sorry, guys, there's nothing to share," Joshua said.

"I can't believe you, man. If it were me, I'd share with you."

"I'm sure you would," Joshua said, though his insult was disguised much better than Jason's.

"Okay, so you're not doing it," Bradford said. "I understand—that would be a sin, right?"

Joshua didn't answer, just turned and started up the ladder.

Jason called out after him: "I hear she gives awesome blowjobs, though, right?"

Joshua looked back over his shoulder.

"Go fuck yourself," he said and started climbing again.

"Come back here and say that!"

Bradford said, "Let it go" or "Let's go" or something like that.

Jason shouted, "Come on, Margolis. You and me. Mano-a-mano."

Then he laughed.

One hundred forty feet up, sweating, winded, and angry—with Jason and himself and Sabrina and the world—Joshua stopped and looked out at the tree tops. The view, framed by the arch of the cave, was indeed worth the climb, he decided, as he slowly composed himself.

He was thinking back to the first grade and being challenged to a fight for the first time. He couldn't even remember the other boy's name.

"Meet me behind the backstop after school," the boy said.

Joshua didn't want to fight, but he didn't want to be labeled a coward, either. He showed up; the other boy didn't. Had he simply forgotten or was he all talk? Joshua realized he could call the boy out the next day, or he could just let the whole thing pass.

Their disagreement, whatever it had been, was never mentioned again.

As Joshua now entered the restored kiva through its roof and descended the ladder into cool darkness, he hoped the same would be true with six-foot-four Jason Castellini.

As SHE WAS getting ready for bed, Sabrina noticed a corner of canvas peeking out from behind her bedroom door. She picked it up, tilted her head, then tilted the painting. The light was no good, so she took it into the kitchen, where she set it on top of the range and flipped the light switch. If she held the painting just right, the two little lights in the hood above the range were kind of like the track lights in a gallery. Again she tilted her head, studying the night-sky painting she had all but forgotten. Slowly, she took a ten-inch chef's knife from the magnetic holder on the wall, plunged it into the canvas and tore a long cold gash from left to right. She put the knife back. Then she whirled and bashed the frame against the edge of the counter, twice, splintering the wood and cracking tile.

"Shit!" she said. "Shit, shit, shit."

There was no one in the house. No one but Sabrina. No one to be shocked by her outburst. No one but Sabrina herself.

It was just a stupid painting. Why stab it to death?

Breathe in, breathe out.

GOING TO THE dentist is never fun, even if the dentist is your dad and he's real gentle with you and doesn't rag on you for not flossing enough. The painful part for Joshua was that he always thought of his mother because she used to drive him to his appointments.

In the waiting room, he'd think of her again because there were copies of *Time* magazine on the table, and she was the one who started the subscription after she found out he was interested in journalism. This was way back in middle school, when his teacher sent home a glowing report of the work he was doing.

He remembered how she started bringing home books she thought he might like. Books that told true stories. Books like *In Cold Blood*, *All the President's Men*, *The Executioner's Song*, and *The Great Shark Hunt*. Books she must have known were intended for an older audience.

The cool thing about his mom was that she had never really treated him like a child, not unless he was sick or injured. Then it was a different story.

But she treated his father the same way.

"Stop coddling me," he would grumble.

But he loved it, and she knew it. They all knew it.

Now, thank God, it was time to go into the back room with the reclining chair, wear the paper bib and the protective glasses, grip the armrests, and close his eyes against the long-armed light. Maybe he would have a cavity and his dad could drill away the decay. Novocain? No thank you.

A few minutes later, his dad came in and sat next to him on the little stool. Then he asked his hygienist to bring him something he'd left in the other room. His dad was not much of a talker, but Joshua could tell he wanted to talk now.

"This woman, Sabrina," he began. "Are you . . . ?"

"No."

His father nodded.

"You're aware of the rumors?"

"Yeah, and so is she. So now we're not even friends."

Again his father nodded and this time patted him on the shoulder.

The hygienist returned.

"Now," he said, "let's have a look at your teeth."

JOSHUA WENT TO the park and waited around the tennis courts every day that week. Sometimes he hit serves, sometimes he didn't. Sometimes he hit against the practice wall, sometimes he didn't. Once he rallied with Tony but they never kept score and Joshua finally showed the poor guy how to hit a solid backhand. After several days, Wheeler showed up with one of his buddies. Joshua got up from where he was sitting on the grass and ran over.

"Wheeler?"

"Yeah, kid."

Wheeler's buddy walked out on the court and started stretching.

Joshua said, "I think I may have given you the wrong impression."

"About what?"

"About me. Me and Sabrina."

"Oh, how's that?"

"We're just friends."

"Just friends. Is that right?"

"Well, we were," he said. "Maybe not so much anymore."

"Why's that?"

"She thinks I gave you the wrong impression, like we were more than friends."

"Not true."

"No?"

"I got that impression from her. From the way I saw her looking at you."

Joshua hesitated, not knowing what to make of that.

"Well, anyway, I let you believe it and that was wrong," he said. "I had no idea the kind of trouble she could get into . . . "

Wheeler unzipped his bag and pulled out a can of balls.

"That's what this is about? She sent you here?"

"No," Joshua said. "This is all me."

"Uh-huh."

Wheeler snapped the can open, peeled off the lid.

"I want us to be friends," Joshua said.

"We are, kid. We're friends."

That wasn't what Joshua meant. He meant Sabrina. But he let it go. He could be friends with Wheeler, too, if that's what he wanted.

"Anyway, I was just trying to make you jealous."

Wheeler chuckled.

"That you did, kid. That you did."

Joshua started to walk away, but Wheeler told him to wait. He rummaged through his bag, pulled out a business card, and passed it through the chain-link fence.

"Call me if you want to play sometime," he said.

SABRINA WELCOMED THE idea of Tara moving in. Though she preferred living alone, it would be a relief to have some help with the mortgage. She might actually be able to put some money in the bank this way. Which is what Tara was hoping to do as well. That and get away from the cowboy who was pestering her.

"I never would have taken him home if I'd know he was going to show up at my door at all hours of the day and night," she said.

AT TAOS PUEBLO, built on the banks of the Red Willow Creek more than a thousand years earlier, Sabrina and Barry paid the fees and signed up for a tour.

Their guide was friendly and the tour informative. The weather even cooperated so Sabrina could take pictures of the pueblo, the creek, and the chapel of San Geronimo (from the outside). But none of it—not even the tasty frybread—made her feel less like an outsider. Because she was. And she was being watched closely.

Sabrina knew from the handout that she was not to take pictures of tribe members without first asking permission, and she didn't.

Their guide said the people in the pueblo live in the old ways, without electricity or running water. They practice their ancient rites and Catholicism as they see no conflict between the two.

On the way back into town, they watched as the wind lifted a tumbleweed over the fence to their right and blew it across the road in front of them. It cleared the fence on the other side, too, just barely, and kept going.

Sabrina asked Barry if he had heard the rumors.

"What rumors?"

"About me."

"That you give the best blow jobs in all of New Mexico? I started that one," he said.

Sabrina punched Barry in the shoulder.

"There you go again, limiting me to regional greatness," she said. "Why do you do that?"

"I told you. That's my frame of reference."

"Anything else?"

"I heard some people saying you aren't fit to sleep with pigs."

"Oh, really?"

"Don't worry," he said. "I stuck up for you. I said you were."

Again, she punched him in the shoulder, harder this time.

"Damn straight," she said. "I sleep with you, you pig."

"I heard the one about you and the kid," he said. "I never believed it."

She kissed his shoulder, rested her head against it.

Joshua was a sweet kid. Reminded her of a boy she knew when she was in high school—Michael Gentry—who had the same expressive face. Michael had been a year behind her, and she liked to sit on his lap and flirt with him because he would blush and stammer. Eventually, he got up the nerve to ask her out, and she could see he was confused and devastated when she said no. She still felt bad about it even now.

"It's a shame," she said. "I liked having him around. Now I can't . . . "

"Why not?"

"I don't want people thinking that."

"To hell with what people think," he said. "Only the truth matters."

SABRINA HAD LOST track of how many times Barry had sat for her. Ten? Twelve? Twenty? He was so patient, so steady, and yet she still couldn't capture the indefinable quality she saw in him. God, it was frustrating.

He'd sit for an hour or more without complaining and love each and every portrait. But each and every one was a failure in its own way. Hell, she couldn't even draw. What made her think she could paint?

This new one, a painstaking pointillist experiment, was pure shit. It was worse than shit. It was shit she had polished into a bright fluorescent stink. She tore it into tatters before Barry could even see it.

He jumped to his feet.

"What'd you do that for?" he asked.

The disappointment on his face made her sad.

"Sorry," she said. "I'm no good."

JOSHUA DIDN'T KNOW what to say when he first heard and then saw Sabrina in the grocery store. You could always hear her coming in her snakeskin boots. Not that other people didn't wear boots, but Joshua must have recognized the rhythm of her walk or something, because he knew it was her before he turned around. He thought she was still mad at him, but she didn't seem to be.

She was with the barrel-chested dude, Barry, the ex-reporter, and she suggested they double date.

"It'll be fun," she said.

"Only one problem," Joshua said. "No girlfriend."

"What about the girl who kept staring at you in the restaurant? Why don't you ask her?"

"In the restaurant?"

"I thought she was cute."

Joshua remembered Sabrina touching his hand, leaning forward, and whispering, "Don't look now, but . . . "

"I hadn't thought about it."

"Joshua, when a girl looks at you that way . . . "

"What way?"

He knew exactly what way, and he had thought about it—more than once.

Sabrina looked him in the eye and nodded.

"I think she has the hots for you."

THE NAME OF the bus girl, which he'd only remembered afterward, was Bailey. Bailey Green. She was a year behind him in school. Joshua hadn't recognized her because she had lost weight and cut her hair, which used to reach halfway down her back. Now it swung just above her shoulders and seemed to suit her better. But it was a shame, in a way, about the weight. She had lost a lot of her curves.

He had heard through Leo (or rather his younger sister) that Bailey was kind of stuck up, but to Joshua she just seemed shy. Shy could seem rude or even conceited if you weren't careful.

In any case, Bailey had eyes that were angelic but sort of wicked, too . . . and Joshua liked the way she looked at him.

He waited outside the restaurant, sipping a large café mocha from a sidewalk vendor, until she showed up for work, then pretended to be surprised to see her.

"Hey, Bailey, how are you?" he called.

She was already in uniform—a short black skirt and white shirt—and looked so dope he got nervous all of a sudden. More nervous than he already was. She was standing in front of him now, smiling, waiting. He took a deep breath.

"Hey, listen," he said. "I was just wondering, um, would you like to go out sometime?"

"When?" she said.

"I mean, not just me. It would be, like, a group thing."

"I'm not working tomorrow," she said.

SABRINA IS CUTTING some guy's hair at the salon but not in her usual chair. It's the chair up front by the window and a crowd has gathered outside.

She is wearing her highest heels, which she never does at work, but they make her legs longer, her butt rounder. She's also wearing a sheer pink babydoll, an outfit she saw in a catalogue recently, an outfit she would never buy. She feels a flood of contradictory emotions—humiliation and pride in equal doses.

Every man who comes through the door asks for her. They're all faceless strangers except for Roger Burnett, her old Hollywood agent, who she hasn't seen in God knows how long.

Juanita tells each man to take off his clothes and wait.

Then Sabrina woke up. She was wet. She couldn't believe she was wet.

SABRINA WOULD HAVE liked to have returned to the same restaurant she and Joshua had dinner in the first time—the place where the rumors were born—but she understood that Bailey worked there and would rather not go back on her night off.

They chose another place, just as popular, and Sabrina made sure they ordered appetizers and salads and entrees and desserts and lingered over a final cup of coffee. She kept the conversation going, asking Bailey about herself, asking about favorite movies and books, about TV shows and current events.

She wanted to be sure everyone had a chance to see that she was with Barry. She even made a point of touching his arm whenever she spoke to him or about him.

Joshua was with Bailey.

Everyone got that?

Good.

THEY DROPPED BAILEY off first. Joshua didn't try to kiss her. He knew Barry and Sabrina would be watching from the car to see if he did, and it made him feel oddly shy. She lived in a small adobe with a porch light that was about fifty watts brighter than he would have liked.

Of course Barry couldn't let it go without comment.

"Lose your nerve?" he asked as Joshua climbed into the backseat.

"Stop it," Sabrina said, butting him with her shoulder. "I think it's sweet."

14

IT WAS ANOTHER sweltering Sunday and Joshua had mowed Sabrina's lawn and helped her weed her garden, along with Tara, who seemed to be living there now.

They were inside now, escaping the sun, and Sabrina was fixing them lunch. Tara had disappeared into the back of the house some time ago.

"Go see what's keeping her," Sabrina said.

Joshua wandered down the hall thinking Tara would be in the bathroom but the door was wide open. Not there. He called her name but got no answer—Sabrina had the stereo cranked up for a favorite Mellencamp song, and he could hear her singing along, loud and off key: "No one wants to be lonely, no one wants to sing the blues."

He continued down the hall. The last door on the left was half open, and when he peered inside, he saw Tara standing in front of a full-length mirror in just her white cotton underpants.

She saw his reflection in the mirror and twisted her torso to look at him. She stayed like that for several seconds. Joshua knew he should look away but he couldn't. Finally she reached for a dress lying on the bed and covered herself.

Joshua closed the door and only then said, "Lunch is ready."

A minute later Tara joined them at the table, having slipped into the clean fresh dress.

"Get a good look?" she asked Joshua.

"Sorry about that," he said.

"Are you? I don't think you are."

Sabrina said, "What are you talking about?"

"Your little amigo here walked in on me while I was changing and couldn't take his eyes off my boobs."

"Joshua! What are we going to do with you?"

He felt the blood rush to his face.

"The door was open," he protested.

Tara said, "I say we take his pants down and spank him."

"Oh, stop!" Sabrina said. "He was only doing what any red-blooded American boy would do, and you know it, Tara."

JOSHUA'S ROOM HAD a hardwood floor, and whenever he couldn't sleep he would kick the throw rug aside and lie naked on the cold boards. It didn't help him sleep, so he couldn't explain it if he tried—it was just something he did that summer.

Sometimes he thought about his mother, but not often. There were good memories, of course, but they only led to sadness, so he avoided them as much as he could.

A tiny woman, Maria Cruz had been working as a maid at a resort in Cabo San Lucas when she met his father, Russell. He knew right away that he would marry her, he said, and he did, two years later.

Now Joshua was hungry for a piece of her blackberry pie. Nobody could make pie like she could, and now there was no pie like hers.

"I learned how to make it in my second year here," she told him once. "A neighbor girl came over and showed me how."

She had watched the girl—"I don't remember her name, but she was a very nice girl"—as she carefully measured the ingredients.

"I couldn't read the recipe. That's why I had to see it—what she put in," she recalled. "That's why I never used a recipe. I couldn't read English."

She tried to teach Joshua but he never got the hang of it, never developed a feel for the dough, and soon—very soon— she was gone.

Lung cancer.

It made him angry now to remember her smoking on the back steps, even after she was diagnosed.

SABRINA SPOTTED A couple leaving their table on the patio outside and asked the hostess if she and Barry could have it.

"Of course," she said. "I'll get someone to clear it."

That someone turned out to be Joshua. As he stacked up plates and glasses, she asked him if he was going to ask Bailey out again.

"I guess so, sure."

"I mean, on your own."

"Sure," he said.

"I really like her, don't you?"

"Yeah, she's great."

"Are you nervous?"

"A little."

He took the dirty dishes away and brought new settings.

"Where are you going to take her?" Barry asked.

"I was thinking of that place on the river. Sabrina, you said you liked that, right?"

"Oh, that's perfect," she said. "What are you going to wear?"

"I don't know. I hadn't thought about it."

"It's a nice place. You should wear something nice."

"You mean, like, my best jeans?"

"You know what?" Sabrina said, "I think we need to do a little shopping, you and I."

COMING BACK FROM the men's store the next day, they were greeted by Tara, who was sitting on the front deck, sipping cerveza from a long-necked bottle.

"What do you think?" Sabrina asked. "Doesn't he look handsome in his new clothes?"

Joshua was wearing a black polo and mud-brown khakis (a combination of what Sabrina called "timeless" designs). Tara looked him over.

"So now he's your little Ken doll?" she said.

"Oh, for godsake, Tara. I gave him a little fashion advice. He has a hot date and wants to look his best."

"Next time, buy tighter pants," Tara told Joshua. "Girls like to see nice butts, too."

"Are you saying I have a nice butt?"

"Get tighter pants and I'll let you know."

JOSHUA WAS SITTING in his convertible, staring up at the sky. He didn't want to get out. Suddenly, Dana Tierney jumped into the passenger seat without opening the door. She wore a white T-shirt, olive green hiking shorts, and tennis shoes, no socks. It was the first time he had seen her since the camping trip. She looked even more sunburned than before. Her hair was almost white.

"Well, if it isn't the incorruptible Joshua Margolis," she said.

"Incorruptible? Why would you say that?"

"I just call 'em like I sees 'em."

"Interesting."

Dana shifted in her seat so she was looking straight at Joshua.

"That not how you see it, Margolis?"

"No," he said.

"No?"

She was smiling a little half-smile, one eyebrow raised.

"How do you see yourself?" she asked.

She was always teasing him, putting him on the spot, making him feel like he was twelve instead of seventeen.

"I don't know," he said. "Not incorruptible."

"So, you are corruptible."

Joshua shrugged.

"Easily corruptible?"

"Well, I'm not sure I'd say easily."

"Wizard," she said. "I love a challenge. So, where are we going?"

Joshua took the key out of the ignition.

"Actually," he said, "I'm just going in to work."

SABRINA WAS TIRED—physically beat from standing on her feet all day, mentally wiped out from too much Tara. A little Tara, she was beginning to see, could go a long way. While Tara was a loyal friend and funny in a shock-jock way, living with her was way different than just being her drinking buddy.

Sabrina had grown particularly weary of the innuendos about her and Joshua.

"How did you feel knowing Joshua couldn't take his eyes off my boobs?" Tara asked her now.

Sabrina just looked at her.

"Made you jealous, didn't it?"

"Don't be ridiculous."

"You covered it well, but I could tell."

Sabrina shook her head.

"Oh, just admit it. You have a mad crush on the boy."

"It's not like that, Tara."

"No?"

Sabrina sighed, sat down, pulled her boots off, and put her feet up.

"I'm very fond of Joshua, but —"

"Fond of him? You're grooming him! The new hair style, the clothes, the advice for the lovelorn—you're creating your own perfect lover."

Again, Sabrina shook her head.

"What do you want to do for dinner?" she asked.

"I'll cook," Tara said. "But, first, just admit—"

"No. You don't understand. Every time I look at him I think of the child I gave up."

"Whoa! You had a child? When was this?"

"I was sixteen."

"And you gave it up, for adoption?"

Sabrina nodded.

"Boy or girl?

"Boy."

"I can't believe you never told me."

"I'm not proud of it, Tara—and don't tell anyone."

Tara stood up, started toward the kitchen, stopped, and turned.

"Do you think . . . "

"What?"

"That Joshua could be your son?"

"No," Sabrina said. "He's not my son."

THE TROUBLE WITH buying new clothes was that it didn't leave Joshua enough cash for the romantic dinner he had envisioned, so he took Bailey for a burger instead. All she ordered was French fries. She wasn't really hungry, she said. He, on the other hand, was ravenous and had a double cheeseburger, French fries of his own, and a peanut butter shake, which he tried to get Bailey to share with him, but she wouldn't even try a sip.

When he took her back to her house, she thanked him.

"For what?"

"I had a good time."

She was standing with her hands clasped in front of her, and he noticed for the first time the tiny paint spot on the hood of her sweatshirt, but he didn't mention it. Maybe she had worn it without knowing the spot was there and would be embarrassed if he pointed it out.

"It must have been fun watching me eat," he said.

"Most entertaining."

"I thought I could make you hungry by savoring every bite."

"It might have worked," she said, "if you hadn't chewed with your mouth open."

Joshua rubbed the back of his neck and smiled sheepishly. Perhaps that had been uncalled for. But Bailey smiled back, apparently willing to overlook it, and when he went to kiss her she did not object. But the more he prolonged the kiss, the more he realized she wasn't exactly putting her heart and soul into it either.

When he pulled back she looked sort of stunned and then she smiled.

He tried again.

Mistake.

THE NEXT TIME Sabrina saw Joshua, she asked him about the date.

"Did you kiss her this time?"

"I did."

"And?"

"What do you mean: And? It was our second date."

Sabrina rolled her eyes.

"How was the kiss?" she asked.

"Okay . . . I guess."

"You guess?"

"It was a simple goodnight kiss, or two, at the front door."

"Making up for lost time, eh?"

She couldn't resist poking him playfully in the ribs. He smiled and twisted away.

"I actually tried to, well . . . use my tongue the second time," he said, "but she didn't open her mouth."

Sabrina tried not to laugh.

"My tongue just flattened on her face," Joshua said.

She touched his shoulder, bit her lip, and tried to look as disappointed as he did just then. His expression reminded her of little Michael Gentry, the boy she had teased so often in school, and it kind of made her wish she had said yes when he asked her out all those years ago.

JOSHUA COULD TELL right away that he was going to spend another punishing night on the hardwood floor. By now he had rolled up the throw rug and tossed in the back of his closet where his father couldn't find it and put it back in place as he often did when he found it kicked over in the corner.

15

SABRINA HAD A booth at the annual art and wine festival—well, more of a white canvas tent—with a dozen of her paintings on display. There were tents just like it all around her in the square. To her right, two women were selling whimsical bracelets. To her left, a man was spinning pottery between sales. Across the way was a photographer whose work seemed to be attracting a lot of interest. Barry was around somewhere hawking the glass creations of the man who was teaching him the trade. Everyone else, it seemed, was a painter like her.

Sitting on a director's chair in the back, out of the sun, Sabrina watched people come through, listened to their comments, and tried to learn what affected them. Was it the painting's composition, the colors, the subject matter, the play of light she worked so hard to capture?

Some loved her work, others clearly didn't. Most came and went without commenting or showing any reaction and that was the most disappointing of all.

She hoped to sell enough to cover the cost of the booth, but so far she hadn't sold anything. Maybe she needed to lower her prices. Maybe she was kidding herself.

"Did you paint these?"

The voice was Joshua's. She hadn't seen him approach. Of course he already knew the answer.

"Hey, there," she said.

There was a handsome gray-haired man with him—an older, shorter version of himself in many ways.

"This is my father," he said. "Dad, I'd like you to meet Sabrina."

She stood up. They shook hands.

"Pleased to meet you, Mr. Margolis."

"Russ, please."

Sabrina smiled and nodded. Russ was her height, as Joshua had been when they met. Now he was several inches taller. When had that happened?

"Sorry about your window," Russ said. "You sure we can't pay you for it?"

"No, no, Joshua has worked off his debt and then some."

God, she hoped that didn't sound sexual.

Russ began to study the paintings.

To Joshua, he said, "You're right. She's very talented."

She sat back down and took a sip of water that was no longer cold. Then she lifted her hair in back so the desert air could dry her sweat-dampened neck.

"What do you call this one?" Russ asked her.

"Awakening."

"Good title," he said. "We'll take it."

RONNI WAS THERE at the festival, alone it seemed, and driving the family car, an emerald-green Buick Le Sabre that was at least ten years old but looked new.

"So your father finally relented?"

"No, he was no help at all. My mother taught me, on the sly," she said.

Joshua watched her bite into a sausage she'd bought from one of the street vendors who had set up shop along the edge of the parking lot. The wind shifted and smoke from the barbecue burned his eyes. Just as suddenly it shifted again.

"You still looking for a job?" Joshua asked.

"Yeah, why? You know of something?"

Joshua was distracted by the stiff empty echo of a paper cup bouncing and scraping across the dusty lot. He turned to watch it pass by, then looked back at Ronni. The expectant look in her eyes threw him for a second.

"You were saying?"

"Oh, um, we had a guy quit yesterday," he said. "Got pissed off and walked out."

Ronni tilted her head and gave him a rueful half smile.

"Sounds like a fun job," she said. "When can I start?"

SABRINA WATCHED JOSHUA finish scrubbing the white walls on her car, using an SOS pad to make them really gleam. Water continued to pour from the garden hose because she couldn't find the nozzle she bought yesterday. Oh well, there was a certain smell to water gathering on sun-scorched gravel that she kind of liked.

"You do good work," she said.

Joshua looked up and smiled at her she walked toward him. She smiled, too, enjoying the soft sway of her broomstick skirt against her legs and the appreciative look in Joshua's eyes.

"Did you sell all your paintings?" he asked.

"You're sweet," she said. "I sold three."

"Only three?"

"One more and I would have broken even."

Sabrina had actually done better than break even but not as well as she had hoped. Joshua just shook his head.

"Who was that girl I saw you with the other day?" she asked. "She's cute."

"That was Ronni, my ex."

"Are you getting back together?"

"Hardly. She's, um, getting to know lots of people."

"Well, you should, too, you know."

"That's what she says."

"If I could be your age again . . . "

"What?"

"I wouldn't take it all so seriously."

"I don't know what she sees in this new guy. He's cocky and rude and full of himself."

"Girls your age—that's what they want."

"Really?"

Sabrina saw the look of confusion on Joshua's face, and it made her so sad so suddenly that she had to blink and sniff and compose herself. What was that all about?

She said, "You could win her back, I bet, if you weren't so nice all the time."

"I don't know . . . "

"I could coach you."

He picked up the hose and took his time rinsing her tires before he finally looked at her and shook his head.

"You don't want her back?"

"Not like that."

Sabrina opened the car door and threw her purse inside.

"Suit yourself," she said.

As she was about to lower herself into the shiny blue Mini, she could tell Joshua was formulating a question for her. She raised one eyebrow and waited.

"What do girls your age want?" he asked.

Sabrina smiled.

"Good question," she said. "When I figure it out I'll let you know."

RONNI FILLED OUT an application. The manager asked Joshua if he'd recommend her.

"Sure."

"So if she screws up I can hold you responsible, right?"

Joshua looked right, then left, as if he were about to bolt for the nearest exit. Just kidding.

"She won't screw up," he said.

TARA CAME INTO the kitchen and sat at the counter.

"Guess who I met today?" she said.

Sabrina gathered three avocados from the window sill where they had been ripening.

"Who?"

"Joshua's father."

Slicing open each avocado, Sabrina removed the pit and scooped the soft green meat into a bowl.

"Uh-huh," she said.

"I knew it had to be."

"They look a lot alike, don't they?"

"I think the dad's a real hottie. A little short, but hey."

Sabrina smiled and shook her head while mashing the avocados into a fine mush.

Tara said, "Like you wouldn't jump his bones if he weren't married."

"He isn't. He's a widower."

"Oh, that opens all kinds of possibilities, doesn't it?"

"Like what?"

Sabrina began chopping the cilantro, stems and all.

"Well," Tara said, "if you married the father, you'd be living with the son as well."

"You have such a dirty mind."

"Think of it. You, my dear, could have the best of both worlds."

Sabrina realized by now that you couldn't encourage Tara, even in jest. If you played along, she'd think you were really serious. If, on the other hand, you attacked the idea, you could be sure she would say she was only kidding.

So Sabrina just laughed and continued with the recipe she had found online for Guacamole Gregorio. A sprinkling of garlic salt, a dash of cumin . . .

16

JOSHUA AND SABRINA were sitting at a small wooden table in her backyard drinking lemonade and iced tea in the shade of a big white umbrella.

She had a stack of magazines there and was thumbing through *Elle*.

Joshua picked up *Vanity Fair*, and on the last page found a questionnaire. He started asking her some of the questions at random.

"What is the trait you most deplore in yourself?"

"Fear," she said.

"What is the trait you most deplore in others?"

"Guile."

"What talent would you most like to have?"

"I wish I could paint."

"But you can," Joshua protested.

"Not as well as I'd like."

"If I could write as well as you paint, I'd be ecstatic," he said.

She smiled and went back to her magazine.

"What is your greatest extravagance?"

"Egyptian cotton."

"Egyptian cotton?"

"Sheets," she said. "Bedding."

"Oh."

He scanned the list again.

"Where would you like to live?"

"Right here."

"Me too," he said.

Sabrina lifted her glass, Joshua did likewise, and they drank to Taos.

"What do you regard as the lowest depth of misery?"

Sabrina looked down and kept looking down so long Joshua thought she wasn't going to answer.

"Not being able to decide," she said.

"Meaning when you can't make up your mind or you don't get to choose?"

Sabrina crossed her legs, closed her magazine (keeping one finger inside), and tucked her hair behind her ear, a gesture that showed off the silver hoop hanging from her delicate little earlobe.

"Yes," she said.

Joshua returned to the questionnaire, reading aloud the first question his eyes fell upon.

"What is the quality you most like in a man?"

"One quality?"

Joshua nodded.

"I don't know . . . Passion?"

Joshua swallowed, read the next question.

"What is the quality you most like in a woman?"

Sabrina stretched and shrugged.

"What do you like most?"

"Passion," he said. "Passion is good."

JOSHUA DROPPED IN for a visit so Sabrina invited him out back where they sat under the umbrella that shaded her new picnic table.

She was going through all the magazines that she hadn't found time to read over the past few months: *Time*, *Esquire*, *Vogue*, *Elle*, *Vanity Fair*, *Travel & Leisure*. Joshua found a quiz in one of them and started asking her about her likes and dislikes, her dreams and desires—the junior journalist at work.

She surprised herself by being frank with her young friend. She may even have embarrassed him a couple of times. He would blush and stammer when she told him about the extravagantly soft bedding she liked or what she looked for in a man.

She wasn't doing it on purpose. He was the one asking the questions; she was just answering truthfully.

It was sweet when he said he liked some of the same things.

SHORTLY AFTER THAT, Joshua came down with something— sore throat, a hacking cough, fever, and sinuses packed so tight he thought his head would crack. The worst of it was over in two days, but during that time he stayed in bed night and day, dreaming fitfully.

He and Bailey are parked up in the mountains, looking down on the town as the sun sets. Suddenly it's dark. The dashboard light is all they have to see by. Bailey's hand is in his pants.

"Whoa!"

Her smile reminds him of a college girl he saw photographed in a copy of Playboy that Leo had once purloined from his father's secret stash. She was peeking out of a pup tent in a pristine wilderness . . .

"What's gotten into you?"

She ignores him, sits back and unbuttons her pants, lifts up, and slides out of them.

"Why aren't you getting undressed?" *she asks.*

"Uhhh . . . "

"Honestly," *she says.* "You act like we've never done this before."

"We haven't."

"What do you mean?"

"I mean we've never done this."

She finishes unbuttoning her top, pauses.

"But Bailey told me you'd done it lots of times."

"You're Bailey."

"You're right. I am. But so is my sister. We're twins."

"I didn't know you had a twin."

"Nobody knows."

She turns her back and, over her shoulder, says, "Are you going to un-hook my bra or not?"

"You have a twin nobody knows about?"

She unhooks the bra herself.

132

"It's easier that way," she says. "I never could have passed trig without her. She never could have passed chemistry without me."

"I don't believe this."

"You asked me out first, but so far you've only been out with her. She always manages to trick me somehow, you see, and she told me you'd done it because she knows how much I want to sleep with you."

"You do?"

"Of course. I've wanted to bag you ever since I first laid eyes on you. Now, just lie back and close your eyes."

"I can't."

"Why not?"

"If I close my eyes, I'll be home in bed."

The next thing he knew that's exactly where he was.

SABRINA WAS SURPRISED that Joshua would share his dream with her, but not too surprised. He was a remarkably open young man. Even so, she could tell—his face was so easy to read—that he was constantly thinking about what to leave out and what to leave in.

"Do you think Bailey wants to sleep with you?" she asked.

"It was just a dream," he said.

"I know, but maybe she really does."

Joshua looked embarrassed.

"Oh, I don't think so," he said.

"Do you want to sleep with her?"

"I don't think we're ready for that," he said. "We're just . . ."

Sabrina waited but he didn't finish.

"You'd like to sleep with her, though, wouldn't you?"

Sabrina was floating backward in her mind even as she looked at him hopefully, wanting him to say . . . what? She didn't know.

"Sure," he said. "I guess."

That wasn't it.

THERE WERE A couple of times when Joshua went down to visit Bailey at the restaurant where she worked and he would order one of the cheaper items—a quesadilla or something. If business was slow, she'd hang around his table and chat with him, one eye peeled for the boss, who liked to say, "If you've got time to lean, you've got time to clean." Then, when it was time for her break, she was allowed to sit with him. But the day after he talked to Sabrina and told her about the dream, he stopped in to see Bailey and couldn't think of a thing to say. She sat with him during her break as usual, and they just looked at each other.

"So . . . "

WHEN SHE WAS talking to Joshua, Sabrina had been thinking of the night she lost her virginity. The boy's name was Danny Fitzgerald and he was eighteen. She was sixteen. The whole thing was her idea, which she thought was outrageously bold of her at the time, though it was probably more or less the norm for the girl to decide these things—let the boy think what he will.

Her family lived in a small town on the Oregon coast then, a town with one decrepit-yet-still-majestic old movie theater, owned by a friend of her father. Sabrina started working there, in the ticket booth out front, when she was just fifteen, with a work permit from the state. By the time she was sixteen, though, she had learned how to run the projector and was locking the place up at night.

It was a choice job because she got to see a lot of movies free, but it also meant she was going to the theater to work when others were going there on dates. Then she came up with the idea of inviting Danny to come in for a private after-hours showing of a movie she knew he wanted to see.

Once the place was empty, she led him up to the musty balcony and told him to take a seat in the back row. Then she went into the projection booth, took off all her clothes, and started the movie. When she came out, she was wearing only her thin polyester dress. Nothing underneath.

She felt naked, but Danny didn't seem to notice. He was already engrossed in the movie as the opening credits appeared and vanished, appeared and vanished.

Taking the worn velvet seat next to his, she snuggled close and rested her head on his shoulder. Slowly, she ran her hand over his thigh. He was starting to get the idea, she could tell, but he just kept watching the big screen.

Finally, she said, "Are we going to do it, or what?"

Not subtle, but effective.

The problem, of course, was that the seats in a movie theater, especially an old theater, are small, and when she straddled him she banged her knees on the metal undersides of the folded-up seats on either side of them. Danny had to scoot out as far as he could, which helped, but she got the feeling that it was the movie, and not her, that kept him on the edge of his seat.

He held her tight but didn't go in for the long kisses she wanted.

She hoped Joshua's first time (she was quite certain he was a virgin) would be better than hers.

She hoped, at the very least, that he wouldn't have to take a stiff brush to whatever surface they chose—which was how she had removed the last traces of her balcony tryst with Danny.

JOSHUA CALLED WHEELER and they met at the park. They rallied and Wheeler taught him that the best way to come to the net was to wait for a short ball so you were already moving forward and didn't have far to go. Just like that you'd be on top of the volley.

Then somehow they both ended up at the net in a rapid-reflex exchange that Joshua would have won if he hadn't missed wide on the easiest shot of them all—a high forehand just waiting to be crushed.

"You see Sabrina much?" Wheeler asked.

"Once in a while, sure."

"She still painting?"

"Yeah. Yeah, she is. Great stuff. Amazing really. She sold some, too, at the art festival."

"Really? Damn! I knew I should have gone to that."

"Why didn't you?"

"I had to be out of town," he said. "Besides, I don't think she really cares to see me anymore."

"How do you know?"

"I don't really. Why? What do you think?"

Joshua shrugged.

17

After a suitable time had passed, Sabrina asked Barry to sit for her again. But, after only half an hour, she stopped.

"This isn't working," she said.

She let him see the portrait this time.

"Am I really that good looking?" he asked.

"Ha!"

The face she had painted looked nothing like his. It was deformed. Ugly. Hideous.

"I am beyond frustrated," she said.

Tears were welling up in her eyes.

"Look," Barry said, "if it pains you that much just . . . "

"What?"

"Nothing."

"No, tell me. Just . . . ?"

Sabrina blinked away the tears, cocked her head, and waited.

"Just, I don't know, try something else."

"Something else?"

"Yeah."

"Like what?"

Barry was silent. He shrugged and looked away.

"I don't know," he said. "Whatever."

"That's great, Barry. Very helpful. *Muchas gracias.*"

"Don't get pissed at me now."

"No? Why not?"

"Because, Sabrina, I'm just trying to . . . "

"What? Finish a sentence?"

Barry looked at her like she was being really unfair, which only pissed her off more because he was probably right.

"I don't know what to tell you," he said.

"You've told me plenty already, thank you very much."

"I just . . . I don't like to see you this way."

Tears were welling up in her eyes again, tears of rage and self-pity, tears she was not about to let him see. She attacked.

"So I should just quit."

"You could, if . . . "

"I should just give up the one thing I'm passionate about, is that it?"

"No, if painting is what makes you happy, then . . . "

"But you think I'm wasting my time."

"No! I never said that."

"Well, it sure as shit sounded like it to me."

Sabrina folded her arms and stared at Barry, who gave her a pathetic, bewildered look.

"Listen, Sabrina . . . "

"I could be a late bloomer, you know."

"I know. Just . . . Take a breath, okay?"

"Fuck you, Barry."

"That's not fair. You know it's not. You never told me how much—"

"I shouldn't have to tell you."

"I don't read minds, Sabrina. How was I supposed to . . . "

"Oh, God, you don't know me at all, do you?"

She turned sharply, strode down the hall, entered her bedroom, and slammed the door.

But Barry didn't leave. He waited for her to calm down, as she knew he would. Then he entered quietly, entered slowly, entered tenderly.

JOSHUA WOKE UP with the sun in his eyes. The sun and tears. The sun because he had forgotten to close his blinds, the tears because of some long-ago sadness he could hardly remember— a dream already forgotten.

DURING A QUIET period at work, Juanita asked Sabrina if she ever thought about trying to find her son.

"Who told you I had a son?"

Juanita cringed.

"I'm not supposed to know that, am I?"

"Who told you?"

"Uh, I probably shouldn't say."

"Look, there's only one person I've told, so . . . "

"Oh, God, he told me not to tell anyone."

"*He* did?"

"Uh-huh."

"Well, the only person I told was Tara."

Again, Juanita cringed.

Sabrina liked Juanita, which is why she kept working for her even though she could probably make more money elsewhere, but this was bad. She had been fool enough to think Tara wouldn't talk, but Juanita? Forget about it.

"Listen," Sabrina said, "it's not even true. I made the whole thing up to get Tara off my back about something else, okay?"

JOSHUA BROUGHT A tub of dirty dishes back to the kitchen, where Ronni sorted plates, utensils, and glasses into their respective trays, hosed them down, and slid them into the washer. He had never seen her in an apron before. She looked crazy hot the way the apron framed her butt, tightly wrapped in a pair of low-cut jeans.

"So," she said, "this woman you bought the painting from—she your girlfriend?"

"No, just a friend."

"She's beautiful."

"She's alright I suppose."

"I wish I looked half as good as she does."

"You do."

"Really?"

"Yeah, about half."

"Smart ass!"

Ronni sprayed scalding water on his feet. Joshua jumped back, his shoes soaked.

"Okay, okay, maybe a little more than half," he said.

SABRINA KNEW IT would happen sooner or later, and it did—Tara confronted her.

"Why would you make up a story like that?"

"Why would you tell it when I asked you not to?"

"Okay, I'm a blabbermouth," she said, "but you're a liar."

"I didn't lie to you. I just told Juanita that to stop her from—"

The phone rang—thank God—and Sabrina picked up. It was her kid sister, Ruby.

"Hey, I was just thinking of you," Sabrina said.

"You always say that."

"It's always true."

"But I'm the one who calls," Ruby said.

Phone in hand, Sabrina made her way into the backyard.

"Ah, but I think of you first," she said. "That's how I get you to call."

"What were you thinking?"

"I was just wondering how you are," Sabrina said. "So tell me, how are you? How's Tom?"

"He's great. We're great."

Wind in the trees, tomatoes on the vine, smoke in the air from a nearby barbecue—the backyard was Sabrina's refuge.

"I'm glad," she said.

142

"In fact . . . we're getting married."

"Ruby, that's wonderful! So Tom's the one."

"Yup."

"Congratulations! I'm so happy for you."

"You'll be my maid of honor, right?"

"Of course."

DANA HAD A habit of appearing out of nowhere. Joshua was just walking down the street and suddenly she was there beside him. She must have come out of one of the shops when he was looking the other way.

She put her arm around his shoulder even though she was shorter than he was by several inches.

"How ya doin', cowboy," she said, almost shouting.

He wondered if she might be mocking him somehow, but he put his arm around her waist. No harm in that. Just playing along.

"Fine. You?"

"Just dandy."

Dana was one of those girls who dressed for comfort— usually a T-shirt and oversized hiking shorts—but still looked sexy somehow. She wasn't as cute as, say, Ronni or even Bailey, but that didn't matter. He liked her playfulness, if only he could be sure he wasn't being played.

"The gang is getting together again," she said, still a bit loud. "You coming?"

Joshua couldn't understand why she was talking so loud, but then he noticed the iPod and the ear buds.

"Wouldn't miss it," he said.

Almost before he knew it, she was gone again, though the citrus smell of her lingered on his shoulders.

SABRINA FINALLY WORKED up the nerve to show herself at the Shadow Dance bar again. Well, not show herself. Just show up, take whatever ribbing came her way, and hope her bare-breasted lapse in judgment would blow over quickly.

She perched on her usual bar stool alongside Tara, and Barry served them margaritas, using the good tequila, the 100 percent blue agave, though he would only charge them for the house brand. He didn't bother asking what they wanted.

"Have anything you want to get off your chest?" he asked.

Sabrina rolled her eyes and shook her head.

"Honestly!" she said. "My breasts were out there for all of, what, ten seconds?"

Barry grinned.

"Ah, but we'll all be talking about it for the next ten years," he said.

Tara cleared her throat.

"And we'll never forget who started it all," Barry added.

Shortly after that, Wheeler showed up with half a dozen friends. He caught Sabrina's eye, as he always did, and nodded. She smiled, a little. This was their usual routine. She knew he would come by eventually (just like he did when she was reading that blow-job novel), and he did.

There was a live band playing and they weren't too bad. Sabrina was pretty sure she had seen them in L.A. once a couple of years earlier. They had a chick singer now who sounded like Rosanne Cash, which was cool because Sabrina loved Rosanne. "Her songs take you so deep you think you might drown," an old boyfriend had said. It was true, too. She liked to paint while listening to *The Wheel*, the images in the songs inspiring and informing the images on her canvases.

"You want to dance?" Wheeler asked.

Sabrina looked at Barry behind the bar.

Wheeler said, "You mind if I dance with your lady?"

"Not my property," was all he said.

Sabrina loved to dance, so she took Wheeler's hand and they headed out on the floor. If nothing else, Wheeler could dance—fast or slow, freestyle or formal. Poor Barry had no rhythm at all.

"I hear you had some fantastic paintings at the art festival."

"Yeah, and I sold both of them."

Wheeler laughed.

"You know," he said, "my offer stands."

"What offer is that?"

He twirled her around and her skirt whirled up and fell back down.

"To show your work at my gallery."

"Really?"

She half expected him to add, "If you take your top off right now."

"Yes. All of it," he said. "And don't act so surprised."

"But you haven't even seen what I've been doing lately."

"I have it on good authority that each painting you do is better than the last. I believe those were his exact words."

"Oh, yeah? Who's your authority?"

"A young man with a very good eye."

JOSHUA HAD ONLY himself to blame for the fact that he now saw Ronni practically every day. On the job, it was bearable, but now, on the street, when he wasn't expecting it—could it sting any worse? She was wearing the jacket, the faded denim one she'd borrowed that time she'd come to his house and the weather turned cold. He'd forgotten about that.

Ronni saw him looking at it.

"Oh," she said. "You want it back?"

She started to take it off but he stopped her.

"The wind is picking up," he said. "You're going to need it."

Ronni shrugged and the jacket was back on.

"I'm glad to see you and Dana together," she said.

"Yeah? She's a kick in the pants," he said, borrowing a phrase his father used to use a lot, though not so much anymore.

"You make a good couple."

Joshua didn't know how to respond. He knew his camping encounter with Dana wasn't the reason Ronni had broken up with him, but the two things were tangled up in his mind. Besides, he and Dana weren't really a couple . . . though maybe they could be.

"So, um, where's Bradford," he said.

"We're sort of feuding right now."

"About what?"

Ronni had a hard time answering. It was like she wanted to confide in him the way she used to, but wouldn't let herself.

Then Bradford showed up and said, "Let's talk."

Ronni walked away with him, waving over her shoulder to Joshua.

WHEELER CAME OVER to Sabrina's house and she showed him her paintings. All of them. The most recent landscapes showing Orphan Mesa, Chimney Rock, Red Hill, and Ghost House. The older still lifes, nudes, and self-portraits. The oils, the watercolors, the line drawings, even the charcoals. All the things she had never even unpacked from the day she'd moved here. All the things she feared would disappoint her.

He was incredibly supportive, and when he said he really liked something, even something she had once hated, it suddenly looked much better to her.

"To think, I nearly burned that one," she said.

"Oh, God, tell me you're joking," Wheeler said.

Sabrina shook her head, smiled shyly.

He slapped his forehead, spun around, gestured wildly with his open hands.

"I'm glad you like it," she said.
"I'm glad you didn't destroy it."

18

BARRY ARRIVED JUST as Wheeler was leaving.

"He came to see my paintings," Sabrina said.

"Yeah, right."

"He wants to show them."

"That ain't all he wants, sweetheart."

Sabrina put her hands on her hips.

"Don't you get it? Sabrina, he's just dangling that out there to lure you in."

"So he just wants my body. Is that it?"

"Come on, Sabrina. Who wouldn't?"

On another day she might have smiled at that, but not today.

"It couldn't be that my paintings are good."

"They are. Of course they are."

"Uh-huh. This from the guy who suggested I give up painting altogether."

"I never said that."

"No? That's how I remember it. 'Try something else,' you said."

"Look, you're the one who . . . "

"What?

"Never mind."

"Say it."

"I'm the one who loves everything you do, Sabrina."

"Oh, sure, you love my paintings. You just don't think they're good enough for a gallery showing."

Barry said nothing, which only served to infuriate Sabrina. She knew she was falling into a familiar pattern, saying the same things, having the same arguments with Barry and with herself. She knew she was out of control, out of line, and now out of taunts. Except one more.

"Wheeler does," she said. "Wheeler thinks they're more than good enough."

Barry left then, but she knew he'd be back. He always came back. It would serve her right if he didn't. She knew that, too.

JOSHUA WAS IN a strange mood. The sun was going down, and he was sitting in the backyard just watching the light change. He sat there a long time while the hacienda down the hill faded into black and reemerged as spots of yellow light.

It was his night off and he didn't know what to do with himself. His friends were all working or grounded or out somewhere doing . . . whatever. The house was dark except for the light from the TV. His father was watching a movie they had seen twice before. He had wanted Joshua to watch it with him, again, but Joshua only lasted half an hour. Then he had to step outside.

He thought about Ronni . . . Sabrina . . . Dana . . . and quickly realized that, if he continued, he'd only end up doing something he'd feel guilty about—something he'd been doing far too much of as it was.

It was a long time before he was able to fall asleep, and he woke up in daylight. His throat felt sore and his eyes were wet. He had been reading a letter. Long ago. Far away. Tears spattered the page. His lids blinked open.

SOMETIMES WHEN SABRINA sat quietly long enough for her folded legs to go numb, long enough for the pain in her lower back to fade away, long enough for her mind to quiet down . . . then sometimes she would have the most vivid memories.

This time she was back on Kauai. It was only six o'clock in the morning and already hot when she went to peek out the window and Wheeler said, yes, he was awake, too, and wanted to see the view. She drew back the curtains. On the other side of the sliding glass doors was Hanalei Bay and the mountains beyond, their peaks obscured by clouds. She remembered stretching across the bed on her stomach to take it all in—their first morning on the island. Then Wheeler couldn't resist. He crawled on top, and she smiled as she let him have his way with her.

Later, on the beach, they listened to the whoosh and sizzle of gentle waves that slapped the shore and washed through the coarse brown sand. They were not the first ones on the beach—a lone woman and two other couples had beaten them to it—but everyone was quiet, said good-morning in passing, and otherwise kept their distance.

This was Sabrina's first visit to the islands and it felt wonderful then.

She could see tiny fish in the ankle-deep water that stretched half a mile off shore before it got any deeper, and on the sand little translucent crabs moved like dustballs in the wind. She and Wheeler walked as far inland as the boulders that looked like giant charcoal briquettes. There they watched big black crabs jump from one rock to the next like mountain goats.

The days that followed were wonderful, too.

It became their habit to sleep with the sliding glass doors open wide and just the screen doors closed to keep out the mosquitoes and the geckos. This was purely a practical move—it got too muggy otherwise—but it had its erotic considerations. Sabrina remembered lying naked on the bed with the morning sun and the still-cool air filling the room. Because of the time difference she continued to wake up early, and one morning as she quietly straddled Wheeler, riding him slowly, she looked over her shoulder to see another couple walking up the path to the tennis courts. She stopped.

Wheeler said, "What?"

Sabrina put her hands over her breasts and came.

Without thinking, she was touching them now, lost in the good memories, blocking out the bad.

JOSHUA TOOK BAILEY out for pizza (of which she ate exactly one slice) and then to his house, knowing his father would be out late, this being poker night for him and his buddies.

Penny-ante poker was his father's one vice. "If you don't have at least one vice," he always said, "your virtue becomes a vice"—advice Joshua always suspected he had lifted from some old movie he'd probably seen a dozen times.

The house was dark and the outside light had burned out so Joshua had a little trouble fitting his key in the lock.

"It's a four-star movie," he said, "according to the guide."

Once inside, he motioned for Bailey to sit down on the couch, and she did—but on the edge, not leaning back. That should have told him something—it did, actually, but he chose to ignore it.

"Looks like it's started already," Bailey said.

"I was afraid of that. Want something to drink?"

"No thanks."

He was thirsty, so he went into the kitchen and pulled a bottle of Coke out of the refrigerator, twisted the cap off, and returned to the living room. The cold carbonated liquid burned his throat when he swallowed.

"What time did this start?" Bailey wanted to know.

He sat down beside her.

"Nine o'clock, I think."

"And what time is it now?"

He glanced at his watch.

"Quarter after."

Bailey grabbed his wrist and looked for herself.

"Nine-twenty," she corrected. "We've missed the first twenty minutes."

"Sorry," he said. "The pizza took longer than I expected. You want to see what else is on?"

"No, this is fine."

He put his arm around her shoulder and she leaned back slowly, keeping her eyes on the set.

"Maybe we can still figure out what's going on," she said.

They watched the set for a while, and then he turned to look at Bailey. She looked at him, too, smiled a quick smile, and turned her attention back to the movie. He kept looking at her. Then, slowly and softly, he kissed her cheek and buried his face in her hair. When he breathed in her ear, she flinched. He backed off.

"What? What's the matter?"

"It tickles."

Of course, it was supposed to tickle in a pleasant sort of way.

The show was called *Vanilla Sky*, and Wheeler had told him not to miss it, but Joshua was having trouble concentrating. His mind was filled with images of Bailey: Bailey in a super short skirt. Bailey in lace panties. Bailey as he'd never seen her.

During a commercial break, he took her chin in his hand and kissed her on the lips. He broke off briefly but then kissed her longer and harder. She let him, but she didn't put anything into it of her own—his big complaint with her.

When the movie came back on, Bailey pulled away.

"Have you figured out what's going on yet?" she asked.

"No," he said. "Have you?"

154

"I'm not sure."

The next thing he knew the credits were rolling and Bailey was doing her best to explain the plot to him.

"Don't you get it?"

He shook his head and watched her lips move. He felt needy and foolish—exposed somehow and yet ignored. How could she not know how much he wanted to kiss her, hold her, feel her next to him?

Finally he realized she was waiting for him to say something. "Hmm?"

"Never mind," she said.

He was in a fog. When she stood, he stood. He was about to make a fool of himself, and he knew it, but he went ahead anyway. Brushing his hand through her hair, he took Bailey by the neck and guided her face to his. Then he slid his hand down her shoulder and over her breast—soft and round under her T-shirt, cupped firmly by her bra—as if by accident.

She caught his hand and lifted it, and for one crazy moment he thought she was going to place it back over her breast. But she just wanted to look at his watch.

"I need to get home," she said.

HE DROVE HER home and stopped the MG so that the passenger door would open onto the stone pathway that led to her front porch. Bailey pulled the chrome lever and the door swung out. He didn't move. She hesitated.

Joshua, who normally walked her to her door, looked straight ahead, kept the motor running.

"Do you want to talk?" she said.

He turned to look at her and shook his head.

She pulled her right foot back into the car and closed the door.

He kept his hands on the wheel and looked off to the left. Under a streetlight on the corner, a gray cat with white paws scurried across the street.

Bailey didn't say anything and neither did he. He wasn't being stubborn; he just didn't know what to say.

He heard the door open and close again.

SABRINA AND TARA were sitting in the two Adirondack chairs out front, drinking a pinon coffee they had recently discovered.

"My little sister is getting married," Sabrina said.

"That's great—isn't it?"

"My little sister, Tara."

"Yes, I heard you."

"My little sister is not supposed to get married before I do."

Never mind that Ruby would no doubt invite their father to the wedding. They were still close, Ruby and Dad, despite the damage he had done. Sabrina couldn't think about that.

Not without visualizing that cliff in Zion.

Not without feeling herself fall the way her mother did.

"Ah, well," Tara said, "it's not like you don't have any prospects."

"Huh? You mean, Barry? Barry is not going to marry me. He thinks I'm stuck on Wheeler."

"Are you?"

"No. Maybe. I don't know."

"Wheeler would marry you in a heartbeat."

"He actually did ask me once."

"Really? You never told me that."

"No point. I said no."

Just then Joshua rolled up on his bike. The two women fell silent.

"What's going on?" he asked.

"Just another beautiful day in the neighborhood," Sabrina said.

But her friend couldn't leave it at that.

"Sabrina's just found out her little sister is getting married," Tara said, "while she, the older and more beautiful child, has no prospects."

"I'll marry you," Joshua said.

"See. Problem solved," Tara said.

Sabrina smiled. With his new hair style, the boy was no longer quite so boyish. He looked almost manly just now, and dead serious, which made his sudden offer deeply touching.

"You're sweet," she said.

She could tell Joshua was offended, but she had to leave it at that.

19

JOSHUA HAD NEVER been to Bradford's place. The front door was wide open, as were the windows, and he followed the sound of music and voices into a huge central courtyard. There he found the gang from the student newspaper standing next to a kidney-shaped swimming pool surrounded by dozens of giant plants—yuccas, agaves, aloe vera—in terracotta pots.

Shakira was singing *"En tus Papilas."*

Joshua had come from working the dinner shift so it was already late. Beer was flowing from a keg in the corner, and people were showing the effects.

The first person to approach him was Dana.

"There you are," she said.

The first two buttons of his shirt were open; she opened the third.

"Where have you been?"

The fourth . . .

"I've missed you, Margolis."

The fifth . . .

Joshua kept backing away slowly until he bumped up against a wall.

He looked at her; she looked at him. She almost spilled her drink. Then she laughed, handed it to him for safekeeping, and went into the house.

He wandered out by the pool, where Bradford was holding court. Ronni was nowhere to be seen and he wondered if that was significant.

"Hey, dude," he said. "Settle a debate for us. What, in your considered opinion, is the best war novel ever written?"

He didn't know why Bradford kept asking him these questions. He was never happy with the answers Joshua gave.

"*Harry Potter and the Deathly Hallows?*"

"Funny. No. Try again."

Joshua thought back to their American Lit class.

"You mean, *A Separate Peace?*"

"That's not a war novel. Come on."

Of course it was a war novel even if the boys were far from the fighting, but Joshua let Bradford's comment pass.

"Not that Hemingway thing you were showing me."

"Killer book, but no."

Bradford kept looking at him, seeming to expect the right answer to come out of his mouth any second, as if this were something they had discussed and agreed on earlier.

"I don't know. What else is there?"

"Hello, um . . . *Catch 22?*"

"Hmm, haven't read it."

"Are you kidding me? You have to read it, dawg. It's fucking brilliant."

"Okay."

"I'm serious. You'll laugh your ass off."

"What there is of it."

It was Dana again, back from wherever she went, her ever-sunburned skin glowing red and giving off heat as she stood next to him.

"Hey," she said, "did you know Bradford is writing a novel?"

"No kidding? That's awesome."

"Well, I hope it will be. I've only just started it."

Someone nearby asked what it was about and Bradford fumbled to explain.

Dana whispered to Joshua, "You should write a novel."

Before he could answer, she was waving to her BFF, Carly Sanchez, a feature writer who wrote Boy of the Month and Girl of the Month profiles.

"I'm burning up," Carly said. "Let's swim."

"I didn't bring a suit."

"So what? We'll swim in our underwear. Same difference."

"I will if you will."

"Deal."

Carly yanked off her top, dropped her pants, and dove into the pool. Dana was right behind her.

They swam and shouted for others to join them.

Joshua envied them and suspected that everyone else did, too, but nobody jumped in.

THAT NIGHT JOSHUA lay in bed remembering a game called Shark in which beginning swimmers scrambled out of the shallow end when their instructor came prowling after them. His instructor had been so stunning—blonde and tan—that Joshua couldn't move when he saw her coming at him. He had always been one of the first to get caught.

He also remembered being in a sea of screaming kids, secretly admiring the sexy young lifeguards during his thirteenth summer. If he concentrated even a little, it was just like seeing them in their underwear. Now he had seen girls swimming in their underwear for real and it was better. Carly's had been black, with lace trim, but Dana's had been pale blue and practically translucent in the lighted water of the pool.

It was a long time before Joshua fell into a fitful sleep.

THE LIFEGUARD HAS to wake him. There's no one in the pool. Everything is still.

"The pool's closed for the day," she tells him. "You sure are a sound sleeper. If you want to swim a little more, you can. Amber and I are going to lock up."

"Sure," he says.

He stands, then jumps in quickly without straightening up all the way. He feels like he has a diving board in his trunks. It's about that obvious. He's sure they noticed, because, when he surfaces, they're still whispering to each other.

161

Full-figured Amber glances at him and smiles as she saunters toward the deep end. Her slender amiga steps into the shallow end. Joshua treads water in the middle.

"Hey, there, cutie. We're going to play a game called Shark. You'll be our bait."

The slender shark is coming closer, talking softly, not in her usual "Behave yourself" voice. Her full-figured friend is already underwater, moving silently.

Joshua swims to the side of the pool, climbs over the edge. Before he can take half a step, a hand grabs his trunks, pulling them down, exposing his pale bottom. He jerks free, runs for the locker room, gets cut off. He turns back, but the other one gets hold of his trunks. They're coming down. When he hits the water, they're around his ankles. He tries to pull them on; the slender shark snags them.

"I've got them. I've got his trunks!"

She throws them to her amiga, who is standing at the side of the pool, soaking wet in a black lace bra and panties. Carly? Carly Sanchez? What the . . .

"Hold those, will you? I won't be needing any more help."

Out of breath, Joshua side strokes toward the diving board, excited by the flow of warm water around his body.

His pursuer traps him in the corner and turns him toward herself. To stay above water, he rests his elbows on the edges of the pool. All the running and swimming have drained him. He can't move from his perch.

His captor—Dana!—rubs up against him.

In the distance he sees, not Carly holding his trunks, but Ronni holding his underpants, dangling them from her index finger.

THE DREAM LEFT him frustrated and confused. He hadn't wanted Ronni in there. Who invited her? Then he remembered that there was a real-life parallel of sorts from earlier that summer:

In Ronni's backyard there's an aboveground swimming pool, round and only about three-feet deep. Joshua lets a splash hit him in the face, turning his head only slightly as a reflex.

"You can knock that off anytime," Ronni tells her rambunctious brothers.

Joshua shakes back his hair, not complaining. The water feels fine, not half as chilly as when it came out of the garden hose a few days earlier.

The brothers don't stop.

"I'm warning you," Ronni says.

They are unfazed.

"Alright, you're asking for it," she says. "If you don't cut it out, I'm going to pants you both."

They laugh and hit her with a rapid-fire barrage.

The chase begins.

The boys split up and go over the side, with or without the help of the ladder, then, one by one, jump back in when Ronni's back is turned.

Joshua doesn't move and no one seems to notice him, sunk low in the water, watching, staying out of the way by staying put. It's as if he's a permanent obstacle you have to play around as part of the game: after a while you don't even have to think about it.

Even so, he begins to feel awkward and self-conscious. Somehow he resents what Ronni is doing, though it's clearly all in fun.

He thinks to himself: "Ha! I'd like to see her try that on me!"

Then he realizes that it's true. Literally true. He wants her to pull his pants down.

20

SABRINA LAY IN bed remembering this:

The sun setting on the island of Kauai, an orange glow illuminating the clouds on the horizon. Wheeler on one knee in the sand, a gentle breeze blowing through his hair, his white shirt fluttering like a sail trying to catch the trade winds.

His words carry the scent of rum and papaya. She likes papaya.

The ring is beautiful, elegant, tasteful, everything she could hope for. Sudden tears stream down her cheeks. Wheeler smiles and tries to wipe them away. She shakes her head and pulls back.

In her mind she is saying yes but her mouth says no.

They are both surprised, both disappointed. That much is clear.

Sabrina also feels relieved and suspects that Wheeler does, too.

JOSHUA HARDLY EVER saw Leo that summer, Leo who worked dawn to dusk on his father's farm, but every once in a while he'd drive out there around lunch time with a couple of giant burritos wrapped in foil and they'd go off and sit under a cottonwood for a while.

It felt good in the shade with a nice breeze blowing.

"We should go swimming again," Leo said.

"Definitely."

They each took big bites of their burritos—stuffed with beans and rice and tender, juicy pork—which they chewed in silence.

"You thinking about Ronni?" Leo asked.

Joshua shook his head.

"I was."

"Now that you mention it," Joshua said, "she did look wicked in that silver bikini of hers."

"No kidding."

Leo's phone beeped. He dug it out of his front pocket, opened it, smiled, and put it away.

"So, um, I was wondering," he said. "You have any objection if I were to ask Ronni out?"

Joshua turned away, looked out across the field. He hadn't seen that coming.

"Go right ahead," he said.

"You don't mind?"

"Why should I mind?"

"I don't know, dawg. You sure?"

A gust of wind blew dust in their faces. They closed their eyes and ducked their heads until it passed.

"She's all yours, my friend."

"Generous of you," Leo said.

They both laughed.

"I know she went out with you first, but don't worry," Joshua said. "By now she's probably forgotten what a butthead you are."

Leo smiled.

"Well, she did say she had a good time last night."

DANA AND HER friend Carly were on the patio sharing a giant taco salad as Joshua refilled their water glasses. His hand was shaking, but at least he didn't spill water on the table. He tried not to think about the two of them in the pool, tried to push aside the image of Dana in her underwear. All wet. Laughing.

"So, Margolis," she said, "how's your novel coming?"

"Novel?"

"Yeah, I bet you could do a lot better than Bradford."

"I don't know about that."

"Oh, I think so. Don't you, Carly?"

Carly nodded.

"I'm seventeen," Joshua said. "What do I know about life?"

Dana smiled.

"What do you want to know?"

SABRINA WAS WEARING cutoffs and a tank top. Her hair looked as if she'd just gotten out of bed, and she had no makeup on. Joshua had never seen her look worse, or more vulnerable.

"How have you been?" she asked.

He shrugged.

"You?"

"Alright, I guess. Um, how are you and your girl getting on?"

"I'm not seeing her anymore."

"Since when?"

"Hard to say exactly."

"I guess you and I are kind of in the same boat then, huh?"

"You and Barry aren't—"

Sabrina shook her head.

"No más," she said. "So did Bailey break it off or did you?"

"I did, I guess. It just wasn't going anywhere," he told her.

"You seem a little sad," she said.

"Do I?" Until she said that, he hadn't realized he was sad. "Yeah, well, I wish things were different. But what can you do?"

She said, "I liked Bailey, but I guess she wasn't your type."

"I don't even know what my type is."

Sabrina seemed amused.

"Don't worry," she said. "You don't have to decide right away."

He laughed.

Then her expression turned sad and there was a long silence. Joshua had a sudden urge to take her to bed, not take no for an answer. She would open her mouth when he kissed her. She would not take his hand away when . . .

He stepped forward, took her face in his hands, and kissed her full on the mouth. God, her lips were soft. He had never kissed lips like hers. He was so hard now it hurt, and he tried to pull her close.

"Joshua, no."

Sabrina turned her head away, and he kissed her neck. God, it was so warm. He could smell her perfume and feel her hands move up to his chest. He couldn't believe his luck, she was about to unbutton his shirt.

"No," she said.

He placed his right hand over her left breast, and could feel her lungs fill with air.

"Joshua!"

He staggered backward and opened his eyes.

She held him at arm's length.

Their eyes met and he could see his mistake.

"I'm sorry," he said.

Her eyes softened then, and although he didn't want her pity, he let her hug him.

SABRINA AND TARA met at the café for drinks and sandwiches that they ordered at the counter. Sabrina ordered first, and Tara said she'd have the same.

"Again, the same?"

"It's my new policy," Tara told her. "You know I always regret it if I don't have what you're having."

Out back they found a table in the shade of the aspen, and Sabrina kept looking around until Tara busted her.

"Wondering whether Wheeler will turn up?" she asked.

"Well, he was here that time you failed to show."

"Know what I think?"

"Hmm?"

The waiter came and neither woman could wait an instant longer to bite into her panini, each striped with dark diagonal grill marks and oozing melted cheese.

"You and Joshua should form a pact," Tara said, her mouth still full.

Sabrina swallowed.

"What kind of pact?"

"Well, you're not getting any younger and you don't seem to like your prospects right now, so . . . "

"So Joshua becomes my fall back?"

"You could do worse."

"Brilliant."

"You know he's up for it."

Sabrina took another bite, sat back, and savored the flavor. She suspected Joshua's offer had come out of some essential goodness in the boy, a desire to help, mixed as it so clearly was with a desire for lots and lots of steamy sex. It was a shock but not a surprise when Joshua kissed her. A shock but not a surprise to feel his arousal pressed upon her. A shock and a surprise to dream about it for three nights running.

170

"He's a teenager," she said finally. "He's up for anything with boobs."

"That may be so," Tara said, "but then why does he want your boobs more than mine?"

AFTER WORK, JOSHUA walked, head down, hands in his pockets, to the parking lot. Leo was waiting there next to his father's rusted pickup.

"What are you doing here?"

"Picking up Ronni."

"Ah. Of course."

"Hey, I saw Bailey the other day," Leo said, "I think you hurt her bad, dawg."

"Why do you say that?"

"I don't know. She seemed really sad. Does it surprise you?"

"Yeah, actually, it does. I'm sorry if I hurt her, but she sure puts on a brave face."

He felt as if he'd made a mistake. Bailey was a sweet girl. Maybe he should call her, start again. But he knew he'd only end up doing more damage.

Then Ronni was there, happy, smiling, oblivious. She got in the pickup with Leo. So much for any girl choosing Joshua over his friend.

The funny thing was it didn't hurt anymore. Just like that. For no reason. It stopped hurting. Maybe he was stronger than he thought.

Ronni was wearing the denim jacket again and Joshua asked for it back.

"Really?"

He nodded and she took it off, handed it to him.

Leo said, "Wasn't that your mom's jacket?"

"So?"

Leo shrugged.

"Just saying."

JOSHUA WENT TO the grocery store to stock up on the Hungry-Man TV dinners he and his father depended on most nights. He found Tara, who worked there as a checker, taking a break outside.

"Would you really marry Sabrina if she wanted you to?" she asked.

"Kind of a moot point, isn't it?"

"Not really."

"I'm too young for her. She's made that clear enough."

"Now you are, sure, but things change," she said.

JOSHUA AWOKE IN the middle of an erotic dream. Other guys his age had wet dreams, but he always woke up before he reached that point. If he wanted release, he would have to take matters into his own hands, which always left him wracked with guilt. But the image was so clear, clearer than it had any right to be: Sabrina, naked, on her hands and knees, looking back at him over her shoulder.

"I can't fight it any longer, Joshua. I want you inside me."

He closed his eyes and tried to ease back into the dream, tried to fall asleep again where he had no control over his actions. It was no use. He got up and walked around the house in his underwear, in the dark, silent as a submarine. He sat in the recliner, he stretched out on the sofa, he stood by the window. Then he went back to his room and lay down on the hardwood floor, more wide awake than ever.

THE NEXT TIME Joshua played tennis with Wheeler, they started doing a drill where Wheeler would grab three balls from a full bucket he brought with him. The first he would hit short so Joshua could come charging up to the net. The second would be low and fast for Joshua to volley. The third, a lob for him to smash.

Wheeler wouldn't try to return any of Joshua's shots; he just stood in place and hit a new ball each time. By the time they got to the bottom of the bucket, Joshua was exhausted. They took a break.

Joshua said, "You're rich, aren't you?"

"What makes you say that?"

"I don't know. But you are, aren't you?"

They sat on the bench beside the court.

"I'm comfortable," Wheeler said. "Why? You need money?"

Joshua shook his head.

"No, I'm comfortable," he said, trying the phrase on for size.

Wheeler pulled two bottles of water out of his bag and handed one to Joshua.

"You want to know how to get rich?

Joshua took a drink and shook his head once more.

"What then?" Wheeler asked.

"Just curious."

"Good, because if you wanted to know that, I wouldn't be able to help you."

"Why?"

"Because I was lucky. I sold a screenplay for a pile of money. My first one, too."

"No kidding? Wow. So did you know Sabrina when she was an actress."

"No, I met her here in Taos, in my gallery."

"Too bad. Maybe you could have written a part for her."

"I wish. I never sold another screenplay, though. Never even finished another."

"How come?"

Wheeler took a long drink and thought for a moment.

"I was really young, too young, and it was all a bit much for me. I let success mess with my head," he said. "Fortunately I invested in some hot stocks and got out before everything went tapioca. Now here I am . . . playing tennis with you."

"You really live a charmed life, don't you?" Joshua said.

"One might get that impression, I suppose."

21

BY COINCIDENCE, JOSHUA and Dana met each other at a drive-in taco stand on Paseo del Pueblo, the main road through Taos, and they sat together drinking fresh watermelon juice.

It was a Sunday afternoon.

"You go to church?" she asked.

"Yeah."

"Why?"

"To worship God."

Dana's phone chimed but she ignored it.

"You don't have to go to church to do that," she said.

"I know."

"Do you think that's what God wants—to be worshiped?"

Joshua lifted his glass, put the straw to his lips, and took a long slow pull. He had never really thought of it like that, but didn't feel like admitting it.

"It's what I want to do," he said.

Dana's phone chimed again and she reached into her bag and switched it off without looking at it.

"You never text, do you?"

Joshua shook his head. How could he text without a cell phone? But he didn't want to say that. It was kind of embarrassing.

"That's good," she said. "My old boyfriend used to text me all the time."

"Was that him just now?"

"That? I don't know who that was. I'll check later. I'm with you now."

Joshua sipped his drink, wondering if she was trying to tell him something. She was with him now, yes, but did she just mean literally with him here at this moment, or—

"You must think I'm awful," she said.

"No. Why would you say that?"

"I don't go to church. I go swimming in my underwear."

Joshua stirred his drink needlessly.

"That's okay," he said.

"You could see everything, couldn't you?"

"Well, yeah."

"And you didn't think to yourself, 'What a slut!'"

"No. Not at all."

Dana's sunglasses kept sliding down her nose and she had to push them back into place.

"Are you sure?"

"You and Carly were just having fun."

"You sure left in a hurry."

"It was late," he said.

"You didn't like what you saw?"

"Actually," he said. "I admired you."

"Did you?"

"Very much."

"Well, don't worry. It didn't show."

THAT NIGHT, JOSHUA got on Facebook and dashed off a private message to Bailey:

JOSHUA MARGOLIS AUGUST 7 AT 11:23 PM

i'm sorry if i hurt you. i know i can come off as a jerk sometimes. it's just that i don't know what to say sometimes. most of the time, actually. you're great, you know. i like you, i do. i even got the feeling that i liked you more than you liked me. maybe you don't like me at all now. i wouldn't blame you. i should have kept my hands to myself. then of course i had to sulk about being rejected when i knew all along it was the wrong thing to do. grabbing you like that. you were great, though. i mean, you did your best to give me the benefit of the doubt and not hold it against me or anything. at least i hope that's right. i just felt foolish and, you know, frustrated. like we wanted different things. anyway, i'm really sorry, that's all.

Minutes later he sent another message.

JOSHUA MARGOLIS AUGUST 7 AT 11:26 PM

at other times, when i look back, i think maybe you liked me more and i just couldn't see it because i'm an idiot with a one-track mind.

Then he started a third message but didn't send it. Why dig the hole any deeper? Bailey never did write back, not that he expected her to.

EVEN THOUGH A part of him still wondered if Dana was only toying with him, Joshua worked up the nerve to ask her out.

"I hear the Fechin House is way cool and I've never been, have you?"

"No, I've always wondered about that place," she said.

When he picked her up two hours later, his jaw dropped.

"What's the matter, Margolis?" she asked. "Never seen a girl in a dress before?"

She was wearing a short white dress with tiny black polka dots, a black leather belt with a silver buckle, and black Dingo boots.

"I've never seen you in a dress before," he said.

Dana smiled, twirled around.

"Didn't think your little tomboy could clean up so well, did you?"

"You look amazing," he said.

"Shall we go?"

As they toured the two-story adobe, they marveled at the detailed carvings and bold paintings of Nicolai Fechin, a Russian artist who spent years remodeling and expanding the house—only to leave it to his wife when she filed for divorce, the tour guide explained.

"This is so totally cool," Dana whispered. "You're the only guy I know who would think of this."

Joshua smiled and shrugged, not letting on that he got the idea from Sabrina, who kept a list of local attractions she wanted to see. (It had been implied that he should join her, as he had at the Kit Carson House, and he would. He'd gladly come here again with her.)

The place closed at five o'clock, so they went for tacos, then ice cream cones, then fancy espresso drinks, and it was still pretty early.

Dana said, "Let's go for a drive."

So they did. Top down, radio up, hair blowing every which way, they sped aimlessly through the streets of Taos for over an hour. He loved how the MG was low to the ground and hugged every curve, how it shifted gears so crisply and responded to the slightest touch he gave the steering wheel. He loved having the top down and seeing the wind play with the hem of Dana's dress.

"Are you looking at my legs, Margolis?" she asked him.

"Busted," he said.

When he finally took her home, she surprised him by inviting him to come inside. He met her parents, which was remarkably not awkward, and before long they excused themselves, leaving Dana and Joshua alone in the living room.

"What do you think your parents are doing?" he asked.

"Oh, they always go to bed early," she said. "They like to read."

Joshua nodded. Dana was sitting really close to him on the sofa.

"What writers do you like?" she asked.

"Depends. What are we talking about?"

"Books."

"Okay," he said. "Nonfiction?"

"Whatever you like."

"Hmm, well, I really liked *A Million Little Pieces.*"

"So, fiction then."

Dana smiled and so did Joshua.

"Right. Good one," he said. "It really pissed me off when I found out Frey made up like, what, 90 percent of his so-called memoir."

"Yeah, but it was a killer story."

"Yeah, I thought so, too—when I thought it was true."

"My dad says there's more truth in fiction anyway."

"How's that?"

"Well, actually, I think his argument is that fiction and non-fiction are more alike than people think," Dana said. "When we can't remember something, we fill in with our best guess—so memory and imagination get mixed together to the point where we can't really separate them anymore."

"Good point."

"Fiction at least acknowledges the use of imagination."

"No wonder you're such a kick-ass columnist," Joshua said.

"Kick-ass, really? You think I'm a kick-ass columnist?"

Dana was waiting expectantly and Joshua felt himself blush.

"Yeah," he said. "Your, uh, your . . . "

His favorite column of hers was a sort of parody of the voting public, a fake news report about a massive revolt in which people take to the streets to demand higher taxes because, you know, war is expensive and you couldn't, in good conscience, pass a huge budget deficit on to whatever might be left of the next generation—the debt would kill them. Somehow, though, Joshua couldn't get the words out.

"You're amazing" was all he could manage.

Dana took pity on him and quickly picked up where she left off.

"Then, like, the writer has to decide, um, what to leave in and what to leave out," she said, "so you never get the whole truth anyway."

"That would be impossible."

"And then, you know, how reliable are the writer's sources?"

"And the writer."

"Exactly," she said.

It seemed like an odd time to get all romantic, but she was so close, and so he kissed her—and she kissed back.

Before long they were stretched out on the sofa together, kissing and sort of dozing. Her lips still felt different, as they had during the camping trip, different because they weren't Ronni's. This time, though, her mouth didn't taste like beer and there was a hint of lipstick with the slippery/gooey feel he liked. He missed the strawberry flavor Ronni's lipstick always had, but he didn't miss it much. He let his hand slide down Dana's spine to the small of her back. She thrust her hips into his. Was she ticklish? He tried it again and got the same reaction.

Dana pulled her head back—for air?—and all motion stopped except for his fingers, then her hips. His fingers, her hips. He paused and tried it again.

She leaned back a little more and said, "If you know what that does to me, why do you keep doing it?"

He felt his face redden and he could not look her in the eye.

She said it like she knew the answer. Like she wanted to make him admit something. Like she was calling his bluff. *I know what you want, Margolis. You're not fooling me.* Like she was accusing him and challenging him in the same breath.

Then she saved him with a hug. *Forget it. It's okay.*

SABRINA AND TARA were sipping margaritas on a terrace over-looking the town square, hungrily awaiting their chiles *relleño*, when they heard the music and saw the MG circle below. The top was down and they could see Joshua behind the wheel. Next to him, a skinny blonde in a short dress crossed her legs and laughed.

"Looks like your boy is having a good ol' time tonight," Tara said.

"He does seem to be enjoying himself, doesn't he?"

An hour later it happened again—the car circled the square, radio blasting, laughter rising to the terrace where Sabrina and Tara were just getting up to leave.

"You wish it were you, don't you?" Tara asked.

Sabrina's eyes followed the tiny convertible and she nodded.

It could have been her.

It could have been her in another life.

Maybe it had been.

Or maybe she was just remembering Wheeler and his convertible.

SABRINA WAS GIVING Joshua another haircut in her kitchen, while Tara sat at the counter sipping herbal tea from a handmade mug.

"So who's this new girl I saw you driving all over town?" Sabrina asked.

"Oh, that's Dana."

"You looked like you were having a good time."

"Yeah, she's fun. I like her," Joshua said.

"No, you *really* like her, I can tell."

Joshua blushed.

"Is it love?" Sabrina asked, immediately wishing she hadn't.

Joshua started to answer, but couldn't.

"Wait a minute," Tara said. "You promised to marry Sabrina."

Now he was really red, and the expression on his face—so serious!—made Sabrina's heart ache for what she couldn't have.

"She's counting on you," Tara teased.

JOSHUA WAS MORE confused than ever. He had gone into his date with Dana thinking of her as his consolation prize, but it didn't feel like that anymore. Could his heart really be that changeable, that fast? Even faster than Ronni's had been, yearning first to be married and then, a few months later, eager to seek out so many other options, so many other possibilities. Only to end up where she started.

22

WHEELER CAME TO the house again and it felt awkward this time. He said it was to see if they could decide on which paintings to display.

"I thought you wanted to show them all," Sabrina said.

"I do," he said. "I do. But it's a small gallery and you have more paintings than I realized."

"I was just kidding. They're not all that good anyway."

He picked up a landscape, looked at it, set it down. He did the same with a portrait and an abstract, not saying a word.

"Let's take a break," he said.

Wheeler sat on the sofa and patted the cushion next to him. Sabrina picked up her sketchbook and sat in the overstuffed chair opposite him.

"I want to do your portrait," she said.

"Not now," he said. "Come sit with me."

She started sketching, but Wheeler wouldn't hold still.

"Stop," she said.

He did, for all of about sixty seconds.

"If you won't come to me," he said, "I'll just have to join you."

He tried to worm his way into the armchair with her, and Sabrina knew it was plenty big enough for two. They both did.

"Don't," she said.

"What? We had some good times in this chair as I recall."

He flashed his boyish smile and Sabrina found that it did bring back fond memories, and yet . . .

"Don't," she said.

"Oh, come on, Sabrina. Lighten up, will you?"

"No."

Wheeler backed off.

"What's the matter?" he said.

"I just feel like you're using this whole thing to see if you can get into my—how should I put this?—my good graces," she said.

"What if I am? Isn't that what people do when they're trying to —"

"To what?"

"To make up for a, for a lapse in judgment."

"Is that what you call it?"

"Come on, Sabrina. Can't you see . . . "

"No. This is not how you make up for that. This cannot be a favor you do to, to . . . "

She was sputtering so bad she couldn't finish her thought.

There was a long, long silence in which they just looked at each other steadily. Finally, Wheeler spoke.

"Are you sure you're ready?" he asked her.

Sabrina shook her head super fast, the way you would if a bug flew into your ear.

"Ready? What do you mean ready?"

Wheeler sighed.

"Listen," he said. "Can you lighten up just a little? Please?"

"No. I won't let you treat me like this."

"Well, what about you? Haven't you been using me?"

"How am I using you."

"To get your show."

Sabrina stood up, red faced. She couldn't even speak. She just pointed to the door.

THE NEXT TIME Joshua stopped by Sabrina's place she wasn't home, but Tara was there—her hair a darker red than he remembered—and she invited him in. She said she had a question for him.

"Do you ever wonder if you were adopted?"

"No."

"Because you and Sabrina look like you could be mother and son."

"You think?"

"You have her eyes and her nose."

"No way."

"Here, look."

She picked up a digital camera that was sitting on the kitchen counter, switched it on, beeped through a bunch of snapshots, and showed him one of Sabrina on the little screen.

"Sorry," he said. "I just don't see it."

"Really? I do. Wouldn't it be wild if it turned out she was your mother?"

"I know who my mother was."

"Are you sure? Maybe you were adopted and your parents never told you."

"Uh, I have to go now."

"Well, good thing you're not going to marry her."

Joshua was making his way toward the front door, but he stopped.

"Look, I know she's older and all that, but she's not old enough to be my mom, and what difference does it make anyway? She's never had a son."

"Oh, I wouldn't be so sure."

Joshua left without another word. Tara was just playing with him the way she always did and it wasn't funny anymore.

HE RODE HIS bike out to the Buena Vista cemetery, where his mother was buried. It was a long ride, longer than he thought. It would have been smarter to drive, but he wanted to exert himself.

By the time Joshua got there, he was dripping with sweat and his legs felt wobbly as he walked his bike along a meandering cement path to the west side. The grave was somewhere in this direction, he thought, but he didn't see it. Maybe he wouldn't. Maybe he didn't want to after all.

He had not been here since the funeral, and the place looked different than he remembered it. Not as green, for one thing.

He circled the area where he thought the grave should be four times before he finally found it, marked by a small hunk of granite with her name carved in it. He was surprised to find fresh flowers there. From his father, no doubt.

How often did he come here? Joshua had no idea. He had always refused to go along when his father invited him and he soon stopped asking.

Joshua read the dates on the marker and did the math one more time: She was forty-eight when she died. She had looked younger, though. Much younger. Too young.

He and his father had adored her and thought that she adored them, but the hard evidence said she had not loved them nearly as much. She said she would give up cigarettes, said she had stopped, but she hadn't. He could smell it on her and see the guilt on her face, time after time, when she realized he knew.

Just now he thought he heard a voice. He looked all around but there was no one in sight. He got back on his bike and pedaled away.

JOSHUA WENT TO take his lunch break in the store room and found that Ronni was already there, sitting on a ten-gallon tub of mayonnaise, with a plate of enchiladas she wasn't eating. She barely looked up when Joshua sat down next to her.

"Do you think you look like your mother?" he asked.

"Not really. Do you?"

"No, I was just looking at a picture of her and I don't see any resemblance."

Finally, Ronni looked up.

"You have a picture of my mother?"

"No, my mother."

"Oh."

She went back to pushing her food around her plate.

"You take after your father," she added.

"Hmm, good point. So there's that anyway."

Joshua was wondering how old Sabrina was and if there was any chance she could have known his father back in California. If she really were his mother, it could be a good thing. He could stop wanting her in the way that she didn't want him. Finally. For sure. No second thoughts. He shook his head and let out a sigh, but Ronni never even looked up. Her mind must have been a million miles away.

"Leo picking you up after work?" he asked.

"Don't think so."

"I thought you guys had a standing date."

"I don't think we're dating any more."

"You have a fight?"

"You know me and my big mouth."

"You'll work it out."

"Listen, I hate to ask you this, but would you talk to him for me? I keep texting him, but he doesn't reply."

"Maybe he left his phone somewhere or forgot to charge it."

Ronni gave him a look that combined skepticism and impatience.

190

"Alright," he said. "What do you want me to say?"

"Tell him it didn't mean anything. It was just a random, crazy, random thought."

"A random crazy random thought?"

She nodded.

"What are you talking about?"

"I can't tell you," she said. "He'll know."

SABRINA DROPPED ICE cubes into the two oversized tumblers that Joshua had pulled down from the cabinet. He seemed to know his way around her kitchen now, though maybe it was just that the glass doors made it easy to find things.

"Sabrina?" he said.

"Yeah?"

She refilled the ice tray with water from the tap and was sliding it into the freezer.

"Um, how old are you?"

She turned and put her hands on her hips. Joshua was pouring warm Coke into the tumblers from a flimsy two-liter bottle that buckled in his hands. Finally he looked up.

"What?"

"Never ask a woman her age, Joshua. Don't you know that yet?"

"No. I mean, why not?"

"It's not polite."

"But it's important."

"Why?" she asked.

Joshua didn't answer. He waited for the foam in their glasses to recede and poured more Coke.

"Why is it important?" she asked again.

"Never mind. It's stupid. Totally stupid."

"You can tell me."

"It's just that . . . "

"Yes?"

"Tara thinks you could be my mother."

Sabrina closed her eyes and shook her head.

"That's it," she said. "I'm going to kill that woman."

"It's not true then?"

"No, Joshua, I'm not your mother."

Joshua looked at her and smiled weakly.

"I was afraid you were going to say that."

Sabrina smiled, too, and hugged him.

"I wish you were mine," she said.

He hugged her back and was not the first to let go, but it filled Sabrina with a loneliness that lingered long after he left.

JOSHUA DROVE OUT to the farm the next day and found Leo moving irrigation pipe with three other guys. Leo waved and Joshua waited in the shade of the nearest cottonwood, where he studied a patch of mud that was now dry, cracked, and peeling like old paint. Leo joined him there as soon as he could break away.

"I hear you and Ronni are fighting," Joshua said.

"Not fighting. I'm through with her, dawg."

"She wanted me to tell you it didn't mean anything."

"She tell you about it?"

"No, she just said it was a random crazy random thought and it didn't mean anything."

Leo said, "It meant something to me."

Joshua raised his shoulders, turned up his palms.

"What is going on with you two?" he asked.

"You want to know? Okay, I'll tell you. I was fucking her, or I thought I was . . . "

"What? Wait. You and Ronni have . . . "

"Yeah."

"Since when?"

"Since, I don't know, a while now. And, yes, I used protection. I'm not stupid."

Joshua wasn't thinking Leo was stupid, just lucky, but he said nothing.

"Anyway, I thought I was fucking her," Leo said, "but it turns out she was fucking me."

"What does that mean?"

"She was on top this one time and I said, 'What are you thinking?' because she had this look on her face, you know."

"No. How would I know?"

Leo waved off the question.

"Doesn't matter," he said. "I didn't get the answer I was expecting."

"Why? What were you expecting?"

"Not what she said, that's for sure."

"Which was?"

Leo picked up a rock and threw it at nothing. Then he picked up another and, still sitting in the dirt, threw it twice as far.

"Ha!" he said. "Beat that."

Joshua shook his head but dutifully picked a small round stone and threw it as far as he could. It landed well short of Leo's. That seemed to give his *compadre* some satisfaction, but not much. He was silent for a long while, and Joshua had to prompt him.

"So what did she say?"

Still looking into the distance, Leo finally answered.

"She said, 'I was just thinking how sweet it feels being deep inside you, filling you—"

"You mean—"

"No."

"But she meant—"

"No."

"I'm sure it was just—"

"No. I'm telling you. In her head, I was the girl."

"Whoa, that's just . . . random."

"Tell me about it," Leo said. "Do I look like a *chica* to you?"

SABRINA INVITED BARRY over for dinner, because it looked like he wasn't going to come around on his own this time. She missed him and felt bad and didn't want it to be over between them. He deserved better treatment than he had been getting from her. That much she was sure of.

She had a big pot of chili simmering on the stove and homemade cornbread in the oven—one of Barry's favorite meals—the sweet smell of it all filling the house. Unfortunately she didn't think to hide her latest painting. When Barry saw it, she could tell he recognized the face right away, even if it did resemble broken glass.

"Why are you painting him?" he wanted to know.

Sabrina was grating extra sharp cheddar to sprinkle on the chili.

"Relax," she said.

"I hate to see you wasting your time on that loathsome prick."

"It's just a painting," she said, "and not a flattering one at that."

She had painted the eyes in the bright blue of a dragonfly's tail, which wasn't true to life but added an eerie, unnatural power to the portrait.

"Right. So who's going to want a painting of . . . that?"

"Oh, I bet there are lots of women in this town who would see the—"

"Well, they're all idiots."

"Yes."

"And you're an idiot."

"Yes."

"So what's the point?"

"That."

"What?"

"What you said."

"That he's a prick and you're an idiot?"

Why, Sabrina wondered, did men never know when to stop, when they had already won?

"Are you trying to make me hate you, Barry?"

"No, I'm trying to make you hate him. I did warn you, you know."

"Maybe you should go."

LATER THAT NIGHT Sabrina had a dream that surprised and frightened her . . .

She is bent over the sofa, one arm pinned behind her back. It doesn't hurt. A little more, though, and it would. A quick hand sweeps her dress up around her hips. She feels her underpants rip and rip again until there's nothing left. Just air.

She looks up then and sees Barry sitting in a straight-backed chair, hands tied behind his back, ankles bound tight. There's a blue bandana in his mouth that keeps him from saying anything. Sabrina looks into his eyes. With her free hand, she reaches into the bodice of her dress and frees one breast, then the other.

Barry clearly likes what he sees and then he doesn't.

Sabrina moans as, behind her, someone starts giving it to her, but good.

Barry squeezes his eyes shut but there's no way he can cover his ears.

Sabrina smiles and moans louder.

Finally the sound of her own voice woke her up. She felt cold and pulled the covers up around her.

AT WORK THE next day Joshua saw Ronni first. Her back was to him. He stopped. Though he had stayed awake all night thinking about it, he still didn't know what to say to her. She turned and looked at him, and he saw the beginnings of a smile run for cover.

"Not you, too," she said.

"What?"

"Don't look at me like I'm some kind of freak."

"I'm not. I wasn't."

Ronni went back to washing dishes, her back to him once more.

"I thought you were different," she said.

"I'm not different."

She turned to face him.

"Yeah? Well, I thought you were."

THE DREAM STAYED with Sabrina. She couldn't shake it, and she didn't like it. She was not that girl, not that cold.

She wanted to talk about it, but who could she tell? Not Joshua and certainly not Tara. Could you imagine? Everyone in Taos—all five thousand of them—would know about it in two hours.

Then, Monday morning, her cell phone rang. It was her little sister. Perfect.

She told Ruby.

Ruby said, "Oh my God! Sabrina!"

"It was just a dream, Ruby."

"I know, but . . . "

"But what?"

"I had no idea, you . . . "

"I repeat, Ruby, it was just a dream."

Sabrina stirred Mexicocoa into her coffee, took a sip, and meandered out onto the front deck.

"Who was behind you, in the dream?"

"I don't know. I couldn't turn around."

"But who do you think it was?"

"I have no idea."

Sabrina sat in her turquoise chair and watched a magpie land in her yard. It tilted its head, pecked the ground, and flew away.

"Well, who did it feel like?"

"Honestly, Ruby, you're as bad as Tara."

"Who?"

"Never mind."

"I'm just trying to help."

"I know."

"So?"

Sabrina sighed.

"So, I'm not sure I'd be able to tell the difference . . . "

"But just, you know, emotionally. Did you have a sense of who it might be?" Ruby asked.

Sabrina had the same feeling she had when she woke up tangled in her sheets.

"No," she said.

"Well, who would you want it to be?"

"I'm sorry," Sabrina said. "Why were you calling?"

There was silence on the line.

Finally Ruby said, "I don't remember."

THE NEWSPAPER GANG got together once more that summer, for a picnic. All the usual suspects were there.

Joshua and Dana arrived separately but quickly gravitated together. Dana immediately took his hand, which raised a few eyebrows and made Joshua smile.

"Did you hear about Ronni and your buddy Leo," Bradford asked.

"What about it?"

"Whoa, that's cavalier, dude. Girl fucks a guy in the butt, and you say, 'What about it?'"

"That's not what happened."

"No? That's what I hear."

Joshua looked at Cheryl, who was standing next to Bradford, and knew the source. Unreliable, to say the least.

"Right. With what?"

Cheryl smiled and held up her middle finger.

"Never happened," Joshua said.

"Oh, and you were there, were you?"

"No, and neither—"

Dana jumped in then.

"Who cares?" she said. "What they did or didn't do is between them."

"You all for finger-fucking guys up the butt, are you, Dana?" Bradford asked. "Maybe you could write a column about it."

She flipped him off and walked away. Joshua, a bit uncertain, followed her.

Bradford called out, "Better watch your bum, Joshua."

Joshua went back and stood directly in front of Bradford. They were almost toe to toe. Joshua swallowed and realized he had nothing to say. He took a swing, a badly telegraphed right hook. Bradford easily blocked the blow and knocked Joshua to the ground.

"Sorry," he said and extended his hand.

Joshua got up by himself.

JOSHUA KNEW THERE was more to what happened with Ronni, because Leo had told him about an old photo he'd seen in her family album: Ronni is ten or twelve, dressed in her father's polo shirt and Bermuda shorts. She has one of her little brothers by the arm and he's trying to get away from the camera because she's dressed him up in one of her skirts.

"If I was her brother I would have punched her out for even suggesting something like that," Leo said.

But Joshua wondered if that was really Leo's reaction when he saw the picture. If so, would he still have slept with Ronni after that? Would Joshua, if it had been him instead? Did he still want to sleep with her even now?

"They were just messing around," he said.

"Yeah? That the way you mess around?"

JOSHUA RAN THROUGH the gears, merged onto the highway, and just drove.

Top down, wind in his hair, he drove.

Eyes on the horizon.

He remembered Ronni saying, "If you do, I'll never speak to you." Ronni saying, "Maybe I'm not the only one who needs to work out a few things." Ronni wanting to rewrite the Bible so husbands would have to submit . . .

He was heading south, going seventy, going eighty. He had a full tank of gas. How far could that take him? He tried to think how much cash he had in his wallet, but couldn't remember. Not enough, that was for sure.

He wanted to keep going forever.

Eventually he would cross into Mexico and—here was a random crazy random thought—he could stay with his aunt. Then his cousin, Christina, could ask him again if he'd like to wear one of her pretty dresses. How about the red one? Or would you prefer the yellow? No? Are you sure?

Then would come the knowing smile, the smile that said, You did it before. You liked it before.

He could see that smile even now, as he had seen it on every visit since he was six years old.

One moment of curiosity, one foolish choice—a lifetime of teasing.

Worse: the knowledge that he had enjoyed it.

He had felt . . . pretty.

How stupid was that?

JOSHUA WOKE UP feeling sad. He had been having a dream he'd had before. The one with the tear-stained letter. It felt like long ago. Not just the first dream, which he had all but forgotten, but this one, even though it just happened. He remembered enough this time to know the letter was addressed to a woman, but he hadn't felt as if he were poking his nose into someone else's private papers. Not at all. The message was meant for him . . . her . . . him.

23

SABRINA COULD TELL something was bothering Joshua—it was always easy to tell with him—but it took some coaxing to get it out of him.

"I don't understand," he said.

"Don't understand what?"

He looked so confused and, well, adorable. Then he told her what Ronni had said to her boyfriend. She did not see that one coming.

Although she could remember reading something similar once about a man and woman trading roles in the bedroom—something by Hemingway, of all people—she never expected to be sitting at her kitchen counter discussing such things with a seventeen-year-old boy. She was almost sorry she had coaxed it out of him, but, really, who else was he going to talk to?

"I told you it was weird," he said.

Sabrina lifted her cup and blew on the liquid inside, knowing full well that it was already cool enough to drink. She had done some birth-control counseling as a volunteer in college, but at least then you got some training. Nothing had prepared her for this. She took a sip, she cleared her throat, and she started to wing it.

"When you think about it," she said, "it's not that weird."

Joshua raised his eyebrows and waited.

Sabrina took another sip of tea.

"Think about it," she said. "When you fantasize about sex, you play both parts, right?"

"What do you mean?"

"I do. I plan the guy's reactions. I know what he's thinking and feeling—what I want him to think and feel. I mean, you think about what it's like for the girl, don't you?"

He rubbed his neck, scratched his chin, shrugged his shoulders.

"Look, you want to be a journalist, right? Aren't journalists supposed to look at everything from both sides?"

Sabrina let him think about that for a minute.

"Anyway," she said, "I'd be very disappointed in you if you didn't consider the girl's point of view."

"Disappointed? Why do you say that?"

"Well, if you want to please a woman, you have to consider how she's feeling and what would make her happy."

"Well, when you put it that way."

She saw the beginnings of a smile flicker on Joshua's lips—it was heartening to see his gentle sense of humor emerging from the gloom—and she smiled at him, too.

"Maybe you could teach me," he said.

Sabrina patted his face and wagged her finger, never letting on how that very scenario had become, despite her best intentions, an integral part of her fantasy repertoire. Blame it on all of Tara's outrageous suggestions. Blame it on her frequent frustrations with the men in her life. Blame it on Joshua's dark eyes and crazy persistence.

The young man blushed and cleared his throat.

"So I guess I should cut Dana some slack," he said.

"Dana? I thought we were talking about Ronni."

"Right," he said. "That's what I meant."

Sabrina shook her head.

"Seriously, though," she said. "You guys are using protection, I hope."

"I don't think they make the kind of protection I need," he said.

AFTER JOSHUA HEADED off to work, the evening turned chilly, so Sabrina built a fire in her kiva, the flames burning bright blue from the high oil content of the pinon logs. Then, before she could settle in with a cup of tea, she heard a vehicle coming up her gravel driveway. Peeking out the window, she saw a florist's delivery van.

The driver handed her a long white box with a red ribbon—long stemmed roses, just like in the movies—and left in a hurry, evidently running late with his deliveries. Sabrina sat down to open the little card that accompanied the roses.

Barry is finally learning to be romantic, if not particularly original, she thought.

But the card was from Wheeler—"Forever and all ways," it said.

She threw it and the roses in the fire.

JOSHUA'S GIRL CAME into the salon and nodded toward the WALK-INS WELCOME sign in the window.

"I'm a walk-in," she said. "Make me welcome."

Sabrina recognized her right away.

"Hey," she said, "I know you."

"You do?"

"Sure, you're, um . . . Dana, right?"

"Uh-huh . . . "

"Hi, I'm Sabrina. Joshua's friend."

They shook hands. Dana sat down, and Sabrina wrapped a cape around the girl's shoulders.

"How do you know Joshua?"

"He's never mentioned me?"

"Mmm, no . . . "

At first she thought, How could he not talk about me? He's over at my place all the time. But then she thought, No, he's got it right. Never talk to your girlfriend about another girl.

"Actually," she said, "he broke my window trying to deliver the Sunday paper to the wrong house."

"Oh, right, yeah, I thought your name sounded familiar somehow. You're the one . . . "

"The one?"

"Um . . . "

The girl's sunburned face turned even redder.

"Ah, you mean the rumors. Not true," Sabrina said. "Is that still going around?"

"Not so much anymore. Not that I believed any of it."

"Thank you. I mean, not that he isn't cute and all . . . "

"Why are the cute ones always so shy?"

Sabrina smiled.

"Sometimes I wish he really had done it with you," Dana said. "Then maybe I could get him to make a move on me."

Sabrina's smile got a little bigger. She liked this girl.

"I can tell he's totally taken with you," she said.

Now Dana was smiling, too.

Sabrina led the girl to the sinks in the back of the salon and started washing her hair. She imagined her and Joshua together. *Her* being Dana. Then she was Dana straddling Joshua, riding him slowly, watching his face, the face that never learned to hide a thing.

Dana said, "What are you smiling about?"

Sabrina coughed and started to rinse the girl's hair.

"What kind of cut did you have in mind?" she asked.

"I don't know. I was hoping you might have a suggestion."

JOSHUA DIDN'T SEE Dana or call her for several days after the picnic. He thought about her a lot, but he didn't call her. When he finally did pick up the phone he ended up dialing Wheeler's number instead and asking if he wanted to play some tennis.

"Listen, kid, things are kind of crazy right now," he said. "I don't think I'm going to be playing any tennis for a while."

The next day, though, he saw Wheeler on the court with a very tasty if not very talented young woman in the tightest shorts he'd ever seen.

Joshua didn't say anything, but made sure Wheeler saw him, too, before he walked away.

The girl was really stunning, though. There was no denying that.

After that, Joshua wanted to call Dana more than ever and yet something stopped him. Not "something." He knew what it was. She had taken Ronni's side, instantly, and he wasn't sure what to make of that. He felt for Ronni, he really did, but he could imagine how Leo felt, too. What if it had been him? He and Ronni had almost done it that time. How would he have reacted? What if they had stayed together and gotten married the way they talked about in the beginning?

He was trying to see all sides, like a journalist, like Sabrina suggested, but his head was an echo chamber:

"How about the red one? Or would you prefer the yellow?"

"That the way you mess around?"

"I thought you were different."

"Better watch your bum, Joshua."

He was still bruised from when Bradford knocked him on his ass, and he still cared too much about what other people thought.

He got on his bike and, without really thinking about it, rode out to Sabrina's house. She was just getting off work and seemed glad to see him.

"Guess who came into the salon today," she said.

"Wheeler?"

"No! God, no. You think I'd be excited about that?"

Joshua shrugged, but was glad.

"It was Dana!"

Joshua didn't know what to say.

Sabrina said, "You should call her."

208

"Maybe I will."

"Maybe?"

"Alright, yes, for sure. I've been meaning to."

Sabrina smiled.

"Oh, and when you see her, be sure to tell her you like her hair," she said. "I cut it really short and I'm not sure she likes it."

So he called Dana and asked her if she'd join him for a little picnic of their own.

"Why?" she said.

He hadn't expected that.

"Uh, because I miss you?"

"That works," she said.

When he picked her up, he was surprised—even though he'd been forewarned—by how short her hair was. Well, short on one side, longer on the other. Totally asymmetrical. He liked it, though. It looked rad and he told her so.

"Really? You like it? I didn't at first," she said. "But, you know, I just put myself in Sabrina's hands and she didn't let me down."

Joshua sensed there was more to that last statement than she was letting on, but he didn't press it. He trusted Sabrina, too.

"So where are we going?" she asked.

"You'll see."

Having checked in with Leo the night before, Joshua drove out to the farm and parked under the cottonwood by the secret swimming hole. In the trunk, he had a blanket, plus a bucket of chicken and three sides from KFC. Also a cooler full of soft drinks.

"You think of everything," Dana said.

They spread the blanket under the tree, which reached into the sky and pulled down a gentle breeze, then they both dug into the food and drinks with relish. The sky was blue with puffs of white hanging just above the Sangre de Cristo range in the distance, and the sun glinted off the slow-moving stream at their feet.

"So," Joshua said, "I've been wondering. What's the deal with you and Ronni? I never see you guys hang out together and yet . . . "

"And yet I leap to her defense and embarrass the hell out of you?"

"Well . . . there's that, yeah, but she surprised me, too, one time. I mean, she wasn't mad at all when . . . "

"I know. She told me."

"So, I don't get it."

"Ronni and I were friends a long time ago. Way back in the third grade I used to go over to her house after school and her mom would make us the best peanut butter and jelly sandwiches. I remember she used to wrap them in wax paper when everyone else used plastic bags. Anyway, Ronni and I would take those sandwiches and ride our bikes out to this little stand of trees and eat them there in the shade. We didn't even talk. We just ate in silence."

Joshua let Dana enjoy her reverie for a minute, then snapped her out of it with another question.

"So what happened?"

"Oh, I don't know. It was nothing really. It turned out that we both had secret crushes on the same boy, and one day Ronni said, 'What would you do if he were here right now?'"

"And?"

"And I kissed her."

"You . . ."

Dana laughed and Joshua tried to erase the surprise from his face.

"We would take turns pretending. One day she was the boy and the next day I was. To practice. In case either of us was ever lucky enough to be alone with our secret crush. Then somebody saw us and I had to stop going to her house and we avoided each other at school even though we both knew it was stupid."

"Who did you have a crush on?"

"You would ask that," Dana said.

She pushed him backward on the blanket, and the next thing he knew she was on top of him, straddling his midsection and pinning down his hands.

He didn't fight her. Didn't want to. Didn't need to.

"So who was it?"

"You," she said.

THE NEXT TIME Joshua dropped in, Sabrina could tell right away—he was different. Not in any overt way, but subtly. And then she just knew.

"So, Joshua," she said, "anything you want to tell me about?"

She looked at him and he looked at her. She smiled and he kept a straight face.

"What?" he said.

God, it was so obvious now.

"You call Dana like I suggested?"

"Yeah."

"And?"

"And, um, we went on a picnic."

"And you had a good time?"

Joshua was smiling now.

"Yes, we did," he said. "We had a very good time."

"I'm glad," Sabrina said.

A FEW DAYS later, Joshua had the dream again. He'd had it so many times now it was starting to feel more like a memory than a dream.

As he was waking up, he had the same long-ago, far-away feeling as before, along with an impression—not an image but just an impression—that the letter writer was an old man, an artist of some sort but not successful, not even close. More and more awake, Joshua could not bring back the words in the letter, only the wasted feeling of the dream. She wished there were something she could have done, this woman in the dream, this woman reading a letter that made her cry.

Joshua shook his head, got up, and got dressed. School would be starting in a few days and he wasn't ready for it. So he did what he had done so often that summer when he had nothing else to do and nowhere else to go. He rode his bike over to Sabrina's place.

As he approached the house, he noticed Barry sitting out front in one of the two Adirondack chairs, playing a harmonica. Coasting over the front yard, he came to a stop next to Barry.

"I didn't know you played."

"Not well, as you could hear."

"Sounded alright to me," Joshua said. "Sabrina home?"

"No, she's in Phoenix for her sister's wedding."

"Right. Then, um, why are you here?"

"I'm mourning."

Barry blew his harmonica. It was a mournful sound alright—not so much a tune as a wail that came from somewhere down deep—and Joshua recognized the feeling even if he didn't understand what Barry was talking about.

"I don't get it," Joshua said.

"She's all pissed off at me, and I thought if I just sat here for a while, a solution would come to me."

"What's she mad about?"

"Wheeler was going to show her paintings in his gallery and now he's not."

"Yeah, well, Wheeler's a prick."

Joshua had always liked Wheeler. In some ways he still did. In some ways he kind of felt sorry for him. But his latest assessment? Clearly a prick.

"That," Barry agreed, "is exactly what I said."

"But what's that got to do with you?"

"I told her Wheeler was only trying to get in her pants."

"And?"

"I was right."

"So?"

"So she hates me."

"Because you were right?"

"That and the fact that I was an ass about it."

Barry blew his harmonica again, and then the two of them sat in silence for a long while.

"I have an idea," Joshua said. "What are you doing tomorrow?"

SABRINA FOUND HERSELF alone in a high-rise hotel room in Phoenix with the sun going down. She was still wearing the lavender bridesmaid dress, still holding the bouquet she had caught without trying to.

Her little sister and her new husband were long gone, and Sabrina half-regretted having turned away the attentions of a handsome young wedding guest.

Her father had walked Ruby down the aisle. That is, their father. Seeing him again was not as bad as Sabrina had expected. He looked old and sort of wasted, but happy for Ruby and clearly pleased to be part of the ceremony. Sabrina made an effort to be cordial and it turned out to be surprisingly easy. He was her father, after all, and there were some good memories there, along with the more painful ones. There was the memory of carefully shaving his whiskers every morning after he injured his hand and couldn't do it himself. That had gone on for a week, and he had been proud of her then and grateful. It was the same face now but different, still handsome but more weathered. She wanted to paint him but didn't think she could—his eyes were happy and sad and happy again but still sad. How was anyone supposed to get that on canvas? If she could do something like that she would be great, but she wasn't great.

If she could just stop blaming him . . .

Alone now in the hotel, she surprised herself by calling Barry's number. He could be such a dick, and yet nobody but nobody had his patience, his tenderness when it really counted.

She got no answer and left no message.

The view from her window showed the flatness of the land and the sameness of the buildings. The sky was the same boring blue as the day before.

She had nothing to do.

Nothing to do but drink every bottle of alcohol in the room's minibar.

Nothing to do but eat every overpriced cashew and chocolate in sight.

Nothing to do but watch Comedy Central in the hopes that someone could make her laugh.

As soon as she got home, she decided, she would burn every last one of her paintings. Start fresh. Maybe she would swear off men for a year or two while she was at it. She had done that before, when she was seventeen and pregnant and decided not to carry the child. It had been good for her.

IN THE MORNING, Joshua and Barry walked and drove all over town visiting gallery after gallery, and gallery after gallery turned them away. Sorry, no can do. Thanks but no thanks. Our buyer isn't here right now. Come back next week. Come back next month. It was exhausting and demoralizing, but they kept each other going.

Following a list Joshua got off the Internet, they visited every single gallery in Taos, with one obvious exception.

No luck.

The next day, they drove fifty miles south, telling each other they were sure to find someone with vision and taste in Santa Fe.

They parked next to the old railroad station and made their way slowly toward the town square. There were certainly a lot more galleries—galleries everywhere—but the story was the same. Not interested. Not now. Maybe some other time.

Joshua couldn't imagine doing this alone, couldn't imagine doing it if he were the artist. He was wearing his best clothes, the stuff Sabrina had picked out for him, and Barry looked sharp, too, but they didn't have the right words, the right demeanor. Plus, they were sweating like madmen. It was a hot day and they were walking all over, so of course they were sweating, but it didn't look good.

They didn't know what the hell they were doing, clearly.

Finally, he and Barry walked into a tiny storefront they had nearly overlooked—a very narrow but surprisingly long space on a quiet side street. The slender silver-haired woman behind the counter looked like Emmylou Harris. That's what Barry said, anyway. Turned out she was a huge fan and they both started raving about a CD called *Wrecking Ball* and some guy named Daniel Lanois. Then they were on to Shawn Colvin. Then Rosanne Cash, whose voice was now coming through the speakers mounted near the ceiling.

"*The Wheel*," Barry said. "Sabrina plays this all the time."

"Your girlfriend?"

"Ah, she's the artist we represent."

Joshua took that as his cue to lift up the painting and set it on the counter. Barry pulled back the cover.

The woman said, "It's sublime. How much are you asking?"

"Oh, this one is not for sale," Joshua said.

"But she has lots more," Barry added.

Slowly, the woman stroked her long ponytail.

"I like this one," she said. "What's it called?"

"Awakening," Joshua said.

The painting showed a face, way up close, with a beam of sunlight hitting the eyes. One eye was sort of squinting or maybe winking. The other was open and reflected the light. For Joshua, though, the really cool part was this: While he could never say why, he always felt certain the lips were just about to smile.

"You sure you won't part with it?"

"Sorry, no. But she has better ones than this even. She could fill your whole gallery."

The woman kept admiring the painting.

"I'd like to meet her," she said.

Joshua pretended not to be too excited until they got outside. He could only imagine how stoked Sabrina was going to be.

About the author

Al Riske has worked as a newspaper reporter, magazine editor, copywriter, and ghostwriter. His first book was the story collection *Precarious*, featuring the Blue Mesa award-winner "Pray for Rain." This is his first novel. Born and raised in the Pacific Northwest, he now lives in California with his wife, Joanne, and their dog, Bodie.